The Girl with the Brown Eyes narrates the journey of Bhaumik, the protagonist who passes through a series of hurdles and interventions till he finds the truth. He fights against all odd things in life and comes out of the events that lure him, misleads him and sometimes create an impression of euphoria. Bhaumik Mohanty, the young novelist, has fantastically depicted the story. I wish him a very bright future of letters and laurels.

Chirashree Indrasingh
Noted Poet & Author – *Bengabati Kathaa & Kimbhira Desha*

Very different style, liked the way each chapter is started, with three four lines of poetic spark. The undertone of the story is relevant, good emotional appeal also. The style and the presentation show the unique talent and bright future of the author.

Monalisha Mishra
Eminent Writer & Novelist – *Kete Dura Krushnachuda & Daki Dei Jae Se Chhai*

After explaining all, something was left unsung, making him feel like he had absconded. The forbidden fruit stayed lodged in him, just like Adam's apple. Even after concluding, the author is bound to ink more. He senses a mysterious allure in her captivating, dusky eyes, which stirs waves of emotions within him. Partially complete yet, "Continued…" Perhaps he is waiting for something elusive, like Godot.

Rajat Mohanty
Author – *Kichhi Barsaa Kichhi Trusha &*
Mo Katha Kabitare

This is fantastic! It is unimaginable for an age where Bhaumik has been able to hold onto parallel tracks and multiple characters with a flow that one experiences only at a later stage of a writing career. This novel has more fantastic elements of surrealism and magical realism. I would have finished the storyline in a different way than the author. Still, I realize he is from another generation and is writing something of another genre. I find more meaning in how he has developed and concluded the plots. The sequel looks different from a sequel, as he blended the story independently of his earlier novel. Good to Go, and a brave author indeed.

Satrujit
Author – *Photo & Pachishra Pachash*

The Girl
with the Brown Eyes

The Girl
with the Brown Eyes

Bhaumik Mohanty

BLACK EAGLE BOOKS
Dublin, USA | Bhubaneswar, India

Black Eagle Books
USA address:
7464 Wisdom Lane
Dublin, OH 43016

India address:
E/312, Trident Galaxy, Kalinga Nagar,
Bhubaneswar-751003, Odisha, India

E-mail: info@blackeaglebooks.org
Website: www.blackeaglebooks.org

First International Edition Published by
Black Eagle Books, 2023

THE GIRL WITH THE BROWN EYES
by **Bhaumik Mohanty**

Cover: Bhaumik Mohanty
Interior Design: Ezy's Publication

ISBN- 978-1-64560-420-4 (Paperback)
Library of Congress Control Number: 2023942428

Printed in the United States of America

Dedicated to My old self.

FOREWORD

Magical Realism: Once Again Let's Take the Flight!!

This is Bhaumik's second novel and I am writing this note for the second time to introduce you to his second work, which in my opinion has moved mountains ahead from where he started writing! But this fact of writing a note for his novel again is a surreal phenomenon for me. The author returns back to the same person for a forwarding note is a very rare phenomenon. So, before I start writing what I think about his writing style, plot, and theme, I thought it is apt for me to thank Bhaumik to give me this privilege and I am touched by this gesture.

When I wrote the note for his debut novel, "I Did, Did I' he was experimenting with a certain type of writing and style, and like many teenagers of his time, he was driving a subtle romance in the disguise of a painting- a painting of an imaginary world where everything appeared real and yet there was a certain unexplainable!

He was building his comprehension, structuring the flow, and linking characters with protagonists in an imaginary plane There was a high level of uncanny ability to hold onto the reader's attention through unexpected occurrences. I presume he has inherited this ability from his poetess mother Deepika and maternal uncle poet Rajat. But he deserves to get a higher credit for his own uncanny abilities to project magic in the mundane real world. His ability to build a complex storyline, and break it into simple, metaphorical sketches to drive the reader's attention is very unique.

So what makes Bhaumik's simple and yet elegant writing into a supernatural storyline as a sequel to his first novel- I Did, Did I? It is the genre of the novel that he has selected to continue his craft of building a magical orchestra! It's magic realism and beyond. Magic realism refers to a class of literature with magical and supernatural phenomena presented in an otherwise real-world and routine setting.

The storyline paints a realistic view of the world we live in by adding a cocktail of magical elements- most of the time it blurs the boundary between reality and fantasy. So how different it is from fantasy? Magical realism has a larger element of the real world and uses magical elements to make a point about the real world. It projects an evolving world. Fantasy as a genre has either no or lesser amount of real world. In this novel, the protagonist has moved from place to place, space to space, and place to space at no time- so fast that the person from the normal, real world will find it as absurd.

The novel depicts a situation where a highly realistic and detailed setting is preoccupied with something that is too strange to believe. Probably the success of the first novel has made the author more creative and braver to imagine and reflect the supernatural occurrences as routine phenomena.

Many marvelous and unimaginable events occur as the narrative moves on. In this novel, the fantastic, unimaginable is happening in the real world. I can say that certain sections of the novel are pure bliss and a part of hallucinating realism. The novel focuses on the actual existence of things and yet takes the reader to sub-conscious reality. Can I name this style of hallu-graphic?

To take the conversation further, I am of the view that this sequel goes one step further where the author combines magic realism with marvelous realism to bring the 'aha effect' very quickly. The author presents fantastic occurrences like teleporting or time-machine mobility in a realistic tone.

This novel blends supernatural realms with a natural familiar world. I have a perception that while writing this novel, the author drove his imagination through the obvious streets, riding on the magical wings through authorial reticence. He applies, hybrid, multiple planes to connect the protagonist with the situations and characters. Over the years, Bhaumik has mastered the art of heightened attention to mystery.

There must be a reason why the author decided to name and end the novel the way it is at the time of publication. I quote Garcia Marquez 'My most important problem was destroying the line of demarcation that separates what seems real from what seems fantastic' (Unquote).

I have a strong feeling that Bhaumik as an author has built his repertoire toward this magical realism. I wish him many more successes and hope he will continue to write in this genre he has chosen so far.

I congratulate him along with his parents Deepika and Kamalakant who are my friends for promoting Bhaumik's creative acumen and writing.

I am sure, like me, many readers will enjoy reading this novel and experience the flight to a different, unbelievable, and fantastic world that is blurred by magical realism.

Dr. Tapan K Panda
Founding Trustee and Chair,
Tapasya Foundation

PREFACE

First were the lucid dreams that were somehow linked to a bigger picture. Say it the numerous clashes between reality and the psychological perspectives or the one between fate and love, once something is written, that makes it unchangeable. All for one and one for all, there's a person who adds the 'may be' to every chapter.

A person who sees,

A person who perceives,

And the same one to whom we are bound forever.

I hope to finish this one better, or someone else will. Who knows. This might be the beginning of a 'may be' or the end of one too. As, if something soars, it drowns too. This is the time when I got out of my loop.

But was that worth it?

I hope someone does get my diary. It was a gift from someone special. Who was it, what happened, and everything related to it is in this diary.

How about we figure things out together again?

ACKNOWLEGEMENT

The writing was always the thing that has and forever will fascinate me. Not just because it is rewarding when it fills out, but it also makes it easier to know what to expect.

This sequel being the second book, makes it a special one for me. The one who couldn't have made it to you all if it wasn't for the unconditional support of my parents. My epitome of love and affection, Baba and Mummy.

I express my utmost gratitude to Sruti for being there as emotional support in every step of mine, backing me up with the serenity of her soul, and to Rahul (Lipun) bhai, my elder brother, who will never leave my side despite the adversities. A special thanks to Tapan Uncle, who has forever been an idol for me in my writing and visualization stages. There are no words to describe what he does to encourage me with my passion.

Remember my favourite person, who was and will always be there for me, right here, at the moment, Grandma.

Chapter: 1

(1 or 31? Well… I leave that to you.)

It was already dawn when the flight landed with the usual thud. Well, I like to call it a dream breaker. Haha. You know every time there's a smidgeon of confusion when you are in a drowsy state of mind, the feeling which you get when you wake up from your pleasant sleep.

In my opinion it is pretty much the best feeling, you know, to be unknown about your surroundings but be able to live the moment peacefully. The avian fluttering of eyelashes, the gentle blink towards consciousness, c'mon isn't that serene? It took me around fifteen to twenty minutes to walk out of the exit gate of the airport.

The temperature was close to 5 degrees. This time cool breezes welcomed me to the new city. A city of hope, where I thought the new thesis of our team would get things done.

"Bonjour, my friend. You are finally here!" someone said from behind. To my surprise it was actually Sruti, remember the team I mentioned? "Hey!"

I said with a giggle. "Blame the turbulence." I added. "Huh! Turbulence? You come here after two weeks of your promised date and you're blaming turbulence for it?" She said. "I know, calm down please. There were things to be done before leaving." I said. "It's alright, I'm just a bit tired of waiting for so long." She said. "Wait, you were here all night?" I said. "Uh… yeah, I thought waiting here for you will be more interesting than the field study that we are doing right now." She said and yawned. "Wow! You never changed." I said and we both smiled.

The colourful giggles stopped after a while. It wasn't like dropping the situation off directly, it was more like a gradual pause, a pause which seemed heavenly. We were just looking at each other for a while, no words, no actions just simply living in the moment. "Ahem!" Yeah, I did that. Now the moment was over, we tried to distract each other with other things but we both knew we wanted to be in that moment forever.

We took a cab and went to our studio. It took us an hour and a half to reach the destination. The cab stopped in front of a building, though it was huge but it was pretty obvious that the structure was very old. "That's a really nice renovation." I said. "Yes, just as you like it. Pinch of modernity in a well-built classic manor" Sruti said.

"I won't say that it is well built or something. It's …" "C'mon, don't be so judgmental." She said before I could finish. "Aye" I said. She smiled and started crossing the street. "Hey! At least help with the luggage." I said.

"Oh! My bad, I am completely used to just run

towards the studio knowing that the team member I like being with is not here." She said. "Whoa! I'm here, and I'm sorry for not being here earlier. Now will you please stop the taunting?" I said. "Apologies! Umm… it feels great when you apologize." She said and laughed. "Humph! Pardon my recalcitrance, your majesty, am I nominated for the 'forgive him' ceremony?" I said. "Yes! You are forgiven." She said and we burst into laughter again.

"Let's go meet the team mates." She said. "Ah! I'm so excited to see our team." I said. "What!? You didn't say that to me in particular." She said. "Oh c'mon! I missed you more than the team." I said in my defense to avoid pissing her off.

We went directly to the studio which was a few blocks away from the manor which was allotted to us for our stay.

"Hey look who's here! Welcome home Bhaumik." Auromic said when I entered the studio. Everyone seemed very excited to see me and seeing our team, all of them, it felt like I was home again. We chatted for a while about the site details and the statements.

You know there's always a philanthropist in every group? Not the ordinary one but an overly excited one. Yes, you guessed it right! It was Sruti.

"Hey guys! He just landed, let him take some rest. Come Bhaumik let me show you your room." She said. "What's there to show? It's just in front of yours Sruti." Deepak said and everyone started laughing. I could clearly see the redness in her cheeks, she was blushing uncontrollably but she still waited near the door for me to catch up.

We went outside, and she started walking briskly. "Hey! It's okay, they were just being sarcastic." I said. "I know that and I am also aware that I'm being a bit too much lately." She said. "No! There's nothing too much in this. That is the whole point right? You want me to be there for you. And you know what? I am here, standing with you… standing for you." I said.

There was an awkward silence after this conversation, she was just looking at me, as if she was looking through me. We reached the manor. "You know what? You have the most beautiful eyes." I said. "C'mon Marshyy, that's a really old pickup line. Try something else." She said and giggled.

I smiled back and said, "Your hands look too heavy, let me hold them for you." "Pickup lines 101? I have read that too." She said and we both laughed at my innocence. We went in and headed straight to the stairs.

It was like a huge staircase that led us to a section of space which had just two rooms and they were right in front of each other. "This one is yours. I mean officially. But you can use the other one if you like." She said and smiled.

It was just us and the beautiful scent of the lilac that filled that space with a beautiful vibe.

It was her.

Sruti, her smile and the vibe around her is so beautiful that quite a times I feel she's the one.

It was night already when I finished unpacking my stuff. It was a gentle knock at my door that made me conscious about the time.

I opened the door… "Bhaumik, c'mon it's dinner time everyone's waiting at the dining hall." Sruti said and entered before I could even say something.

"Okay, let me just…" Before I could finish my sentence she held my hand and took me with her.

I saw our whole team at the dining hall. Everyone was waiting for me. "Sorry guys… I didn't check the time." I said and sat on one of the chairs.

Though I was enjoying my dinner and was a part of the discussion that was going on, what I could only think of was the playfulness of hers. The way she cared, the way she looked at me, was she the one?

We finished our dinner and headed back to our rooms. It was a dimly lit hallway with antique wall lamps giving out an ambient spell of citrine. It was just me and her walking up to our rooms which were just in front of each other. She was finely dressed in a pastel pink gleaming like a diamond even in that lighting.

Yes that was her, the woman that I fell for. I kept on looking at her. Her charm, her beautiful eyes, the way she smiled and the way I felt when she was around, everything about her made me fall in love with her in every fraction of second. Even the look she gave when she caught me looking at her for some time, that cute face takes away all the thoughts and puts up just one and that's her.

Wait! She just did that, Ah! She knows I'm looking at her, She started to smile. There's a thing about her when she smiles at me about something like this.

She starts to move fast as she knows I'll catch up with her. "Hey! wait for me!" I said. "Catch me if you can sweetheart." She said and started to walk fast. "Oh c'mon!" I said and started to match her speed. It was that moment then and it was this moment now, we were running past the hallways giggling around the whole manor.

Our laughs, smiles and innocence filled the manor, which was silent for ages, with love and playfulness. Soon, both of us stopped running. "We are out of shape." She said while she panted. "That's just us growing old, Muffin." I said and held her shoulders with both of my hands. "Aww, it's been ages since I heard that name. I missed you so much Marshyy." She said emotionally. "Hey! It's okay, I'm here now. Come here, give Marshyy a hug." I said, wiping the tears from her red cheeks.

She pulled me into a tight hug and snuggled. "I missed you too, I'm really sorry it took me so long to reach here. Hey, how about a coffee date tomorrow? You know, as compensation?" I said and smiled. "Just like college days?" She said and smiled. "Yes Muff, yes… just like college days." I said and hugged her.

It had been years since we met. The last time was

supposedly when we completed our masters. I still remember she had burst into tears when she had to move here, to Switzerland permanently. Even though we were in the same firm, we got the leads from two different places. Hers, Switzerland and mine, South Korea which were geographically the almost opposites. Daily meetups turned into video chats and coffee dates that both of us loved were long discontinued.

The only thing that held us together with this distance was our unconditional love for each other. It was a year before this day that I got a notice from our firm that I had a chance to move permanently to Switzerland to work alongside her as the office here in South Korea was being shifted back to India. The first thing I did was to call her and tell her about this, she was really happy, we both were.

And now I'm finally here, here with her, here with us.

Chapter: 2

Sometimes a single word can bring up a thousand smiles and the same happened with us. It was like someone painted us with colours of positivity and cheerfulness. I was enjoying this, the people, the work and not to mention the presence of Sruti.

Time passed by in addition to moments where I and Sruti were like two people who wanted each other's company every time and wanted to live in our moments, frame by frame.

It was the weekend again. We had completed our site visits and case studies. By this time we had a few days of rest before the next project analysis.

Sunset has a different kind of feeling when you are peacefully sitting in a studio which is far away from daily traffic noise and has a beautiful hillside view. The sky, the sunset, the openness of mind, the slow music playing.

Wait! Music? Turning away from my thoughts, I noticed Sruti was sitting just beside me and was playing soft music on her phone. "Hey! I didn't realise you were here." I said. "Of course, I didn't want to break the flow of emotions that you were having seeing the sunset outside. So I thought of playing something to intensify that feeling." She said and smiled.

Her smile. Ah! That sends shivers down to my spine. It gives me out a beam of light to my soul, guiding it to pass through the darkest shafts towards love, and by love, I mean her.

"What are you thinking?" She said. It was pretty obvious because I was just looking at her right after she smiled.

"Ahem… Nothing." I said. She smiled again. She knew that she was the one whom I described indirectly as my reply.

"You are like to ice and I to fire. How come it then that you could be so great, are not dissolved through my hot desire?" She said. "Haha, Sonnet 30 by Edmund Spenser? Read that." I said and laughed. She made a face, an innocent one. "It's not just you, I read books too. Haha." I said. "Haha… very funny." She said and made that face again.

"Hey you two love birds! C'mon we are having a movie night." Auromic said to us. "Seriously Auromic? You and your childishness." I said. "What? Movie night isn't childish, and if you are complaining about being called love birds, then that's your fault pal." He said and laughed.

"Typical Auromic!" I said and shook my head. "Blah… blah… blah… Now c'mon!" He said. "Alright!

Wait for us." I said. "Okay!" He said while he was going downstairs.

"Shall we?" I said and stood up. "Can't we stay like this forever? Being here seeing the stars meet with the skies and just being there for each other?" She said. I didn't have anything to say. I was just frozen. *"Did I hear this clearly? Did she say that?"* This was all over my head.

"Awe, look at you. Don't think so much. I know you want that but I also know it's not possible. Let's go." She said with her smile.

She stood up. I was still frozen in my thoughts and was looking at her with a surge of emotions.

"Oh c'mon! Don't be so sweet, you're making it harder for me to get past that point." She said. Somehow I got out from that surge and looked down to cut eye contact.

"Yeah! Everyone's waiting for us. You go first, I'll catch up after locking the studio." I said. "What? We are going together. I don't want you to get lost finding your destination." She said.

"Did she mean she is here to guide me in every aspects of life?"

"Yes." She said. "What?" I said. "I mean yes. I am here for you if you are thinking that right now." She said.

"How is that possible?"

I wasn't saying all this. I was just thinking and she interpreted it.

"Now stop thinking, let's go!" She said.

"Ye… Yeah!" I said.

We closed the doors and windows, locked the studio and were ready to leave in the next five minutes. "Things are so easier when you are with me." She said. "Just a helping hand. You know?" I said and laughed.

"Okay, now stop calling yourself that, you mean a lot to me." She said. "Whoa! Okay your highness." I said in a sarcastic tone. I saw that innocent face again. The way she does that, to be honest, my heart melts.

"Stop that!" I said. "Stop what?" She said.

"Stop making that face." I said in a lower tone. "Why? You don't like it?" She said and intensified her looks and made that face again.

"It's making you look cuter and I can't resist that!" I said in a higher tone and realized I shouldn't have.

"Awe, you think I'm cute huh?" She said and smiled.

What? Obviously I couldn't say anything.

"Your silence says it all, you have just booked an unlimited pack of that look. Now I have an advantage." She said and grinned.

"We are getting late." I said and looked straight to deviate myself.

"Are we?" She said and did that again.

"No!" I said and closed my eyes. "Closing them

won't help. You'll see me either way." She said and giggled.

By the time we had reached the manor. I didn't say anything. As I knew she was ready with the response. She was still laughing.

"You won't close the entrance?" She said. "Oh! Yeah, I forgot." I said and turned.

She was just standing there, looking at me, smiling. I closed the door and went back in.

I saw her changing to that face again and before she could I started running towards the living area. "You can't run away. Haha!" She said and laughed. "We'll see" I said and laughed too.

Both of us reached the living area, panting. "Are you guys alright?" Deepak said. "Yeah" we both said. "Just a race!" She added.

"Alright! Now c'mon, the movie is starting!" Ayushman said.

We watched the movie, it was actually a movie marathon, pretty boring to be very honest. They'd put up an action genre.

I thought of an idea, a childish one but it could be only accomplished if it was done along with someone, and hopefully, that someone knew I was coming up with it. How do I know that? Well, she was already ready and was looking at me before I turned towards her.

"Let's go!" She said with a gesture and extended her

hand towards me. While everyone was busy watching the movie, two kids held each other's hands and went out to see life by themselves and live it. Okay, I know I'm exaggerating this but for us it seemed like skipping the growing up stage and going back to our childhood.

"Did someone notice?" She said while she was out of breath from all the laughing and running away.

"I don't think so. But yeah let's get away from this place before someone actually does." I said and before I could do anything, she put up her palm on my mouth as I was about to laugh pretty hard and loud as well. Well eventually I did but by that time I had taken her hands in mine and we ran outside the manor to the portico that she had designed. Both of us were looking at each other and were smiling at our childishness. It was under an old Rhododendron. The whole garden was filled with greenery and was lined with orchids, daisies and lilies; It felt as if our fantasy that we wrote in our diaries came into life.

"We never changed." She said, still looking straight into my eyes.

"And never will." I said looking at her beautiful eyes. A strand of her hair had loosen down from her bun and was hanging right in front of her eyes. The way she looked, the way she smiled, the way I felt about her, her, me and this moment, everything. I was really grateful that we were right there with each other.

Sitting there under the night sky, just us and the wind, our moments, our eyes locked into each other; this whole ambiance is what we missed for years. Holding each other's hands, looking through ourselves, all these years, all these emotions, everything that was suppressed for quite long, came right in front of our eyes. Time had healed the pain, it was time which caused this present to happen.

We could hear the soothing sound of dripping water, it had started to rain, a gentle yet mesmerising pouring. A rhythm of nature, a note to love musical, the rain had added just the aura we craved for ages.

Dimly lit faces under the dark skies,

Gaze locked within themselves,

The same rain,

The same people,

The same feelings,

The same pages,

Yet their love was still new,

Two souls lost within themselves.

She looked down after some time, rubbed her eyes with the sleeves of her pastel blue sweater, the one which once used to be in my wardrobe, my favourite one. She still wears it, ah! this feeling, this closeness, this warmth. I missed all this.

"Hey… sleepyhead, nap time?" I said with a smile.

She smiled and looked at me. I could see tears forming up in her eyes.

"I missed you so much." She said and hugged me. "I know Muff… I missed you too, I missed us." I said and wrapped my arms around her. "Don't cry, I'm back here with you. I won't be leaving Muff." I said and started to gently circling my finger at her back, just down her neck, she liked that a lot.

I saw her go to sleep in my arms with a big smile. Seeing someone you love feel this comfortable with you is what one can ever expect for. Her adorableness could take away all the pain and sufferings that I had faced in years and could fill me with harmony. The peace to my chaos, the reason for my smile. My happy place.

It was quite late and chilly outside, once the pouring stopped I carried her back to the manor. She still held me tight even when she was asleep. When you connect with someone and that connection ties you from within, there's no physical force that can break that connection. One can break a person but can never break a connection.

I reached in front of her room. "Ah! Wait, I don't know the passkey." I mumbled. Every room had a 5 digit custom passkey. I thought for somewhile and remembered one thing, a memory, a funny one and tried to put up the passkey. 'Access granted' It said.

"She still remembers." I thought with a big smile. Right from opening the door, coming in and gently putting her on her bed, everything about her room was about us. Our pictures, the presents we shared, our artworks, everything. She had kept everything with her even the rose I gave her for the first time, it was preserved inside a glass.

The moment I put the blanket on her and when I was about to leave, she extended her hand and held mine. She wanted me to be there with her, even in her subconscious state. I sat beside her holding her hand looking at her beautiful face; my sleeping beauty.

Chapter: 3

A mansion.

A vineyard.

Hazy figurines.

When the quietness filled the azure sky with chaos, I could finally make out that I was on a patio. Looking around wasn't fruitful as that place was completely concealed within a weird looking greenwood.

Following the restless movements, I could see an outline forming up out of nowhere and then came the fear of realisation that it was sitting right in front of me.

An expressionless face

A faceless expression

It's hard to describe what it was but the vibe that surrounded me was purely negative.

"What's going on?" I said.

"Who's there to protect you now? Her love? Do you think so? Try calling her." A voice came from the mannequin.

No sooner than I heard that voice, I experienced a memory, a painful one. No names, no voices, no one, just a feeling, just a pain.

Was it the past? Or was it in the future?

All of it compressed towards the back of my head.

"It hurts!" I said unconsciously.

"It sure will. Let it consume you. Don't resist it. Let yourself to us, you won't regret." It said.

"She can." I said.

"What? You think she can take you from us? You think we will let that happen?" It said.

"Do whatever you can, I know she can. No one else but her." I said.

"Hmph… you chose misery, wraith for you then." It said.

Screams

Louder than one can ever imagine to hear from someone

Shriller than one could ever resist

Pain is constant, the thing that differs for individuals is the way someone suppresses it. For me, it was her love and affection that numbed the abysmal scars of mine.

"We'll take you down. We'll sure do." It's voice started ringing in my head.

The more I tried to run away from it, the more it tried to take me in with it.

My constant attempts were going in vain and I was losing all of it. The moment I thought I submitted to that being, I opened my eyes and saw the inside of my bedroom. I was lying on the bed. My left hand was on the side and my right hand was on the bed, slightly under the pillow that I was leaning my head against. The clock on the wall told me it was a bit past six, already early morning. Where was I? I was in my bedroom, that's where I was. It was still early in the morning.

Looking at the clock and my room and my surroundings, even the first memories came back in my mind's eye. The memories and the emotions I felt years ago were starting to obscure all other memories of the past years. I was eventually able to forget about the recent past and the memories that brought it about but at the cost of the return of the past.

"Good morning Marshyy!!" I heard someone. Breaking the last spell of sleep, I saw Sruti standing next to me pouring a cup of coffee, I looked at the golden liquid, and then back at her. I had a sudden urge to get up, hug her and then be there for sometime so I did. I felt something, a soothing form of purity. A healer to my chaos, she herself was enough for me to calm me down.

"Hey you alright? When I woke up in the morning, I saw you had fallen asleep on the side couch by my bed." She said and hugged me back.

I didn't say anything. "Don't worry you don't have to. I know what's going on. Those nightmares of yours, they're still haunting you aren't they? It's okay, come here, Muffy's here for a hug." She said and held me in her arms.

Scared yet getting past the phase of worries, the warmth, the affection, all of what I craved for years.

"It's okay, Don't worry, I can!" She said.

At this moment I knew why she was here. I didn't ask anything. I just knew. I knew she could help me the way she did back when all of it had started. Back when I was stuck in the loop of parallelism, she was the one who took me out of that loop, a savior.

And there she stood holding me in her arms just like the way she did back then. It was still there, her magic, her love, her presence that made me feel like home.

"My home." She said. I could feel warm tears flowing down through my cheeks, she felt them too.

"Listen, get ready." She said. "What?" I said. "No questions, just get ready." She said took me with her.

"What's your passkey?" She said. "You already know it dear." I said with a gentle smile. "Wait! Seriously?" She said and started putting up the code. She knew both of us shared the same passkeys and remembered that moment when I had come up with that idea while setting up our computers back in college.

'*Access granted.*' It popped up.

"Oh my God! Marshyy remembers. Should I be surprised?" She said and giggled. "That's a fine question, Should you?" I said with a smirk. "Hahaha, very funny, had it been something else other than this, you would have missed the opportunity for a date with the queen." She said. We laughed.

Yes, we never changed…

We entered my room, it was pretty dull as compared to hers. I mean yeah, I just came here but still I had managed to give that blank room a touch of mine. "Now let's see what this mister has to wear to go out with the queen." She said while opening my wardrobe. "See it for yourself." I said.

"Oh my God! You still have it?" She said while pointing at a pendant, the one she gave me on our first date. It was actually a part which would become 'one' when the one she had was placed next to mine; A yin yang.

"I had said that I would never ever lose it, right when you gave it to me." I said with a big smile. "Aww, that's so sweet, wait is that…" She was about to say when I said, "What? Is that the cute monkey keychain that you gave me? or is that the chalk you carved 'love' in for me? or are those the marbles that you gave me? Oh wait, did I forget the shells that are just by the side? Remember them?" I said.

"You… you still have them? I gave them to you. It's been more than 12 years. You still have them!" She said in an emotional tone. "What did you expect? I would forget the memories you gave me? I would forget the moments of us? I would forget what we shared right from the start?" I said looking into her eyes. "Remember you said not to wear that pendant more often as I could actually mess up with its beauty? *'Just twice or thrice when we are together and on a nice occasion'* Remember saying that to me? I said and giggled.

The moment I finished saying that, she turned towards me and hopped on me and wrapped me in with her legs on my waist, pulling me into a tight hug. I wrapped her, putting my arms around her.

"Aww my sweet lil' Muffyy." I said. "You're mine, you're here, please don't go." She said in a quiet emotional tone. "Never again Muff, never again. I'm all yours." I said and hugged her tight. "Now let's see what I can wear for the date?" I said and looked at her. She smiled.

The moment when I was about to put her down, she said, "Whoa! whoa! whoa! What do you think you are doing?" "Putting you down? I guess?" I said. "Na-ah-ah, you can't do that, you need to take my permission before doing that. Na-ah-ah, you stayed away for this long, now carry me everywhere." She said and did her cute little' angry face; closing her eyes shu, squinching mouth towards one side and then turning her face towards the other. "Oh I missed you so much, and yes from now on you're not gonna change this position, stay with me like this, you, me forever." I said and pecked her cheeks. She blushed, I could see her turn red. Haha. She was trying to control her smile while looking the other way.

"Hmm… So let's see what I can wear for going out. How about this one? I said and looked at her. She didn't reply directly but shook her head still looking at the other side.

"Haha… okay how about the one I wore when I took you out for the first time?" I said and looked at her again.

A big nod this time. Haha.

"Aren't you the cutest?" I said and pecked again. "So oldie it is." I added. "Okay so how about we just put you down for a moment and I just change my shirt?" I said. She still didn't say anything and jumped back down just like a child. "Oh good lord, I can never resist her cuteness never!" I said and put up that old shirt which I wore when I had asked her to go out for a date for the first time; a navy blue shirt with lil' white circles stippled all around.

As soon as I finished putting it on, she said, "Aren't you forgetting something?" "How can I?" I said and smiled. "Hop on dear, c'mon, come to Marshyy." I said and she hopped back in. Both of us laughed.

That day, we went out after years. It still felt like the first time, y'know, taking out someone you love for the first time? That feeling? It's like one of the best feelings one can ever experience. We enjoyed ourselves. We enjoyed 'us'.

We went for a long drive, ate our favourite dishes in cafes, went to malls and got disappointed with the tags, just kidding we didn't do that. Haha.

It was like, getting back the colours I lost in my life, she was the one who painted my smiles, the one who brushed out all the lowness, and filled me with unconditional love; a feeling worth living for.

It was already evening and both of us where sitting on the bonnet, looking at the blending of vermilion hues and tints of pink that filled the skies with a charm of it's own and us under the sky, holding hands, looking back at the memories we shared, our moments that we once created and the ones that we were about to.

Her, me and us.

Chapter: 4

Melting hearts,

A one that is in love and the one which is still healing with the beats of the other

The sound of sea waves and the smell of fresh air, peace and tranquility was the ambiance that was flowing inside her.

A happy face.

A moment of harmony.

The way she looked at me, it was as if the atmosphere in the place was met with overwhelming joy and optimism.

… A new dawn to my darkened manifestation. A new perspective. Y'know addiction towards something can be taken away with rehabs and orchestration but when you get addicted to someone's affection, my friend, that's the best bond one can ever think of …

A voice broke the silence of the room.

"That's a great choice of words pal." Someone said.

"It's all about being the rustic feather and ink in the world filled with dreaded blinking cursors." I said.

In the room filled with fake applause I saw a face, an adorable one waiting by the threshold, for me? obviously! Haha

Her mid-night black hairs that flowed over her ears, a strand of them hanging in front of her eyes, the innocent face that she makes when she is nervous, everything about her amuses me.

"You did great!" She said.

"We did great, teamwork is what made this possible." I said.

She nodded with a smile and took me out of the exhibits section. Out of the crowd of hundreds, I could only see her holding my hand and going past the unfamiliar identities.

"You still thinking about them?" She said.

"Uh what? Whom?" I said.

"You know who." She said. "Don't you think after these many years of knowing you, can't I tell what you're thinking." She added.

"I don't know, the more I try to avoid them, they come back. Had there been something that could help me forget the past, I would have given it all I have, just to get through that phase." I said.

We were already outside, by the time I was looking at the project we got into, she stopped and looked at me.

"Marshyy, listen… and listen carefully, all of it, the past you're talking about, the future that you think of with confusion, your thoughts about reality, everything… they're all just memories, phases that you went through and the way your mind comprehended your depression." She said.

"Doesn't that mean, I should be out of them when I pushed myself out of my depression?" I said.

"There are times when you try to run away from the past, but it somehow comes back to you, you shouldn't worry about it coz that's just you helping yourself to get stronger, once the old you sees that now there is nothing that can break you, they'll leave you. Alone but stronger." She said.

"I really hope this turns out the way you're saying it will. Coz I'm done with all this, I lost to the past not once but copious times. I don't think I'll be able to fight back again this time. I chose chaos to control me. They gave me a choice but I chose chaos, and I was the one who let the chaos within me, I was the one who let the chaos scar my face and let itself in. All of it was because I was stupid enough to let this happen to me at the first case." I said.

Having been told all of it in a single stretch, the memories, the emotions, the perspectives and the past, all of it hit me straight on my face, letting me down to the ground.

"Don't say that!" She sobbed.

"Ah… umm… I'm… I'm sorry, I'm really sorry Muffin. I got carried away, forgive me." I said and hugged her.

She hugged me back and it took her some time to stop sobbing.

"Hey let's go back to the manor, we will have a cup of coffee, a coffee date maybe? I'll make Americano for both of us, just the way you liked in college. Hehe" I said.

She smiled while she was still hugging me and nodded her head.

"Ah, there she is, my sweet little Muffin." I said.

"Hey!!! little? Excuse me mister, I'm taller than you. Hymph." She said.

"Yeah… yeah whatever shortie. Haha." I said.

What? You think she's gonna forgive me for that? Haha, I was chased down the road by her. It was a pretty good time to be honest, messing around with someone you love and them, running behind you, filling the world with giggles all the way around.

In the world filled with pretty faces and materialism, I had someone who was beautiful and realistic; a dreamer like me. We ran past the traffic, crossing the trees which were shedding the leaves of love. I was turning back quite a time, and saw her smiling all the way around and running towards me. It felt as if the beautifully toned buildings, the trees that blended in, the vintage cars and cafes, the anonymous faces, everything stood still and it was just us flowing with time, our time.

Time. What an amazing term to describe the way we perceive when things are to be done and how those things change with us, or sometimes change us. In our case, it was always with us and never too. One moment was like

… Wow! That was a great day indeed, we should do this more often but the thing is time will still fly away while doing stuff we love …

And the other was like

… Why is this all so repetitive? Why do we have to argue on the same points every time there's a misunderstanding? …

Right in this moment, time was running slow, it was making us feel what we missed, all those laughs, all those childishness and all those years of being with each other.

"Haha gotcha! You're such a slow coach!" She said after she caught me. "Oh c'mon I stopped for you to catch up." I said and laughed. "Ha-ha-ha very funny, don't try to hide the fact that I can outrun you." She said and lifted her head; the glance of glory. Yep, that's her, my sweet little Muff. Haha

"Aww, shortie won and caught me? How cute." I teased her. "What!? You said what now? Get here mister!" She said as I had already started rushing away.

There was this long road that led to our manor, but there was a small alley where I hid and waited for her to come. I could hear her footsteps. "Marshyy? Marshyy where are you?" She said. I could feel her laugh turn into worry, her voice started to shrill. "Marshyy? Please come out if you're hiding. I'm sorry if I did something, don't leave me here, I know this isn't easy. Marshyy please come back." She said. I could hear her crying. "Hey! hey! hey! Muffy hey! I'm here… don't cry. I was just playing around. Hey!" I said after I ran towards her and hugged her. She was completely in tears. "It's okay… it's okay… I'm here. I'm with you. Muffin, don't cry." I said. "Why would I leave you all by yourself?" I added. "I… I jus… just… It just came up… I don't know why I said that." She said while she was crying. I just stood there holding her in my arms, gently brushing her hairs, while she rested her head on my shoulder and cried.

"I know, you missed me. I know being disconnected for so long might have brought up your old thoughts back. I'm here with you and always will be. I won't let anything take me away from you. It's okay, Muffin." I said.

I still remember these thoughts of her when we initially started talking to each other back in college. Her thoughts were way more powerful and used to take her back to a loop of gloom. She always used to say, hugging me and feeling my presence made her feel herself again.

'A lost connection' that's what she used to call our bond. A tie that was lost a long time ago but the ends met again after years.

"Hey! Let's go back. I bought your favourite ice-cream while I was coming here. "Cookie and cream!" We both said at the same time.

She took my hand and ran towards the manor. Oh my sweet little Muff.

Love.

A belief,

A magic,

A happy place,

An inspiration.

Chapter: 5

… I swung wide the door of my bar, slipped into the darkness, and took my first real breath of the day, too in the smell of beer, the spice of a dribbled bourbon, the tang of old popcorn …

"Seriously, bourbon? Haha… The man who has never drunk anything other than milkshakes, says he knows the spice of bourbon." Sruti said and burst into laughter.

"It's all about expressing the way you feel about your surroundings and not how you express yourself in it. Like how we look at things, we don't see ourselves doing it, we see what the consequences were of what we did." I said.

"Well, if you hit me back with your philosophy, trust me you're gonna miss out on your dessert." She said and winked.

"Oh is it? Eh, I will still get my snacc right? I mean snacks. Teehee." I said with a grin.

"That's not the question, you should be asking whether or not you want it." She said.

"Alright you cheeky minx." I said and started moving towards her.

I don't know whether it was because of us, our playful nature and childishness or if it was a certainty. The way we enjoyed our company, the way we laughed, the way we were for each other.

Whatever it was, it surely was something out of a book, an endless chapter of love.

A bright sunny day,

A beautiful start,

A weather of calmness,

The skies coloured with love,

A biblical harmony.

What's better than a lovely start to a day with your most favorite person?

… I am fat with love! Husky with ardor! Morbidly obese with devotion! A happy, busy bumblebee of enthusiasm. I positively hum around him, fussing and fixing. I have become a beautiful thing. I have become myself…

I saw it written on one of her notes, perhaps a one for me to notice. Haha. Damn she's so cute.

I rushed outside, just a sudden urge to hug her and wrap her in my arms. Soon I was out of my breath. The dizziness took me down. A thick black fluid started to form up against my pupils.

"Am I dreaming still?" I said.

"The question is, are you actually here?" I heard a voice.

The same voice, the same particles, the same vibe.

… Are they back? Am I not here… Thoughts started to form up.

"That was your chance, the last one, you refused it, you chose chaos over peace. Now you shall face the consequences." The voice continued.

"Whatever I did was right, unlike you, I never asked anyone to be one amongst them, it was your choice to choose someone and you made a mistake. I know you can't take me with you as long as I don't allow you to." I said.

"You have changed a lot from last time, what have you become? Jack of all trades but master of none." It said again.

"It's rather incomplete, it's A jack of all trades but master of none, but is always better than a master of one." I saw a light, a hope, someone was there, a pure soul, the one which was capable, the one who actually could take me out of all the miseries.

A hand

An epitome of love

She pulled me out, but for her it was waking me up from my unconscious state.

"Hey!! You alright Marshy? What happened? I heard you coming down but you didn't show up so I thought to check on you. I found you here lying down. Marshy… Are you alright?

"Uh… umm I'm sorry, I think that I slipped down the memory lane again." I said.

"Those things again? Oh dear lord." She said and took me in her arms.

"I'm here for you, don't worry." She said and hugged me tightly.

"I'm really grateful for that." I said and snuggled.

There are times in life of people, when there's only one solution to every question, one feeling for every emotion and one attribute for every consequence;

Love.

Chapter: 6

"Wait, is that a Mazda?" I said pointing to the car that Sruti unveiled from which was disguised inside the bushes.

"Yep, a 3." She said.

"A red Mazda 3. Like, seriously out of all the cars out there, a red Mazda 3." I said with a grump.

"Hey, that's one of my favorites." She said.

"I'm not complaining about that, it used to be my favorite too and I had the same model with the same colour." I said.

"Oh look, we still make the same choices." She said and smiled.

Her smile, really, the most beautiful creation of the almighty, y'know the way you feel when someone you love smiles in front of you and their smile initiates the same within you.

"That's a thing of us that'll never change, the way we perceive things and the way we act on that perception." I said and smiled back.

"But why did you exclaim this with a bit of fright?" she said.

"Umm… uh… Nothing. Just some brain fluid leaking. Haha." I said.

She gave me an expressionless look, a look that someone gives when they know you're not opening up completely. On my side, I knew I shouldn't be thinking about this as a sequel of events which did happen in the past. Or did they? I don't know, I'm not sure. The only thing I know is stuck in my memory, the unstoppable flow of emotions, the endless sorrow that I went through or maybe I think I did.

Thinking is believing. Right?

"Stop it now, you know right I do know what's going in your mind right now." She said.

A face with rage,

Impatient expressions,

Juxtaposing care and aggression,

The belief in him,

The love for him.

"I… c…. can… can't actually stop it, it's the way I have become. A change, an alteration to my real self. A side filled with fear of losing out on everything." I said.

By the time I completed saying I was already weeping.

I never weep,

At least I stopped doing it after what happened in the past. The moment I closed my eyes due to a mild irritation in my eyes, I was back.

Back in the moment where I left. That's what happens every time right? Someway or the other we get back to the place where we started everything. The same restaurant, remember?

... But the thing that wasn't normal was the restaurant. It was no longer the way it was when I came in. It was more debris than furniture. As if it was way too old to be functional ...

Yes, that one.

The one with the dark matter,

The one where I was stuck within me and someone like me,

The one where I came to know the hard truth about the way others see you. Or the way you see them. The transparency between the world of ours and that of theirs.

All of it, kept in the exact same way... The same way I left them there.

"You didn't take a photograph last time, are you ready to take one now?" The same woman whom I met years ago or Did I?

"Remember that quote? It's still there. The one that amused you and led you here last time. Are you still searching for it?" She said.

"Whatever it is that you think I was or am searching for, is wrong, coz apparently I found someone, an unexpected yet unconditional love." I said.

"Love, hmm… quite a big term for you in person to manifest." She said.

"There's nothing small or big in this world, it's always about perspective. How people see things, whether they're seeing a particular thing as a matter of great interest or nothing at all." I said.

There was an awkward silence for a couple of minutes. One could even hear the sound of the air passing through the shafts.

"You sure have changed, the voices were right, you're more powerful than you ever were. Making you the most competent host ever." She said.

"You do remember what happened last time right? You and all of em' were sent back to where you belong." I said.

It takes quite a lot of courage to talk to them… but the past had made me do it, I was no longer a person who feared chaos. And once someone chooses chaos over sacrifice, that's when they decide to take control of their own self.

"Last encounter was a mistake, this one is a consequence, a mere doing of yours." She said.

"My doings? Wait. Wh-"

Just before I could complete my sentence, I felt warmth around me.

A gentle touch,

A serene sensation,

A familiar feeling,

A lovely soul,

My Muffin.

Standing there wiping my tears, completely aware of the happenings, waiting there with a hope of saving me from my thoughts. She started to ring the blues and held me tight to herself.

See?

The only one who can take me out even when I hadn't decided to,

There are certain people who are there in your lives as a part of the almighty, sent to you by them who always try to help you against 'them';

For me it was her;

The moon to my darkness.

Chapter: 7

A snowy afternoon,

Breezes filled with calmness,

Chilly spine?

Naah, not this time.

It was pretty warmed up actually. Hot water bag was to be blamed. Hypnic jerks and weird sleeping positions had been increasing with time.

Why? No idea.

Them? Maybe.

…Am I getting old? That's the phase where everyone feels no pain, or as if they do but it hurts no more? Why is everything a maybe? It's actually true for everyone, we are sad and angry at some point in our lives. That's right ain't it? It's all the same for everyone no matter whoever it is. It's very easy to get angered by something or someone, easier than being sad. But with age we forget the difference, it all seems the same, the anger, the sorrow, the numbness, everything Age is what takes away the innocence within us, when time acts as a person, a person who tries to get you restricted to certain things, a frame, an enclosure …

Well we can't change time, what we can change is what we are doing in it as in what we want to see and achieve in that particular frame. Will it work if I compress it to myself? A sarcophagus?

Am I that old enough to even think about these things? Or is it my other consciousness taking up the decisions for me? My inner self. Or is it the other one who was forcing me out of myself.

Am I still myself? Or is everything happening again? Are they gonna come for me again?

It had been a really long time since I had these kinds of thoughts, at least not after that day; not after what had happened, the past was once again repeating itself.

Was it all a mistake?

Running away from them was actually one of the worst decisions I made?

Was it all about submitting to them?

Was it all about accepting the alterations rather than trying to keep things the way they're, rather than keeping yourself; the innerself alive.

… Suddenly, it was all dark again, but he had enough guts to open the door of the cellar. He could feel an odd sensation within himself. There was an almost painful longing to pull the mask off. He realised that it was just the mannequin which was used by a doll maker. "Who are you anyway?" She asked. It was he, who looked confused. That little girl was sitting with her bowed down head near the mannequin, she was probably talking to something. "Do we have a problem?" She asked again …

"What's going on?" Damn I have to be more conscious about my surroundings, that's like the zillionth time I was thinking this.

... "I said... Do we have a problem?" The little girl shouted and started looking towards me, or the person within which my consciousness resided. No sooner than the girl started grinning, I found the mannequin's head tilted towards me. A faceless grin ...

Why was this mannequin looking so familiar?

Even without a face, how could I make out that it was grinning?

The fact that intimidated me was that this state seemed more real than my actual self.

The fact that I wasn't already out of all this was a matter of fright.

... "Who's there to protect you now? Her love? Do you think so? Try calling her." Someone said, supposedly the mannequin ...

This memory, the pain, was I here before or was this the 'before'? No names, no voices, no one, just a feeling, just a pain.

... "They'll soon be here for you, stronger and soon will be the day when you'll be filled with dread, the dread of losing what you have, the dread of losing what you are. Soon will be the day when you'll no longer be mortal yet will die everyday, chaos will consume you. Soon will be the day when there won't be anyone to take you out, soon will be the day when no one will remember you." It said ...

"No! no! stop it! Please… someone stop this!" I yelled or that's what I think happened.

… No longer a human, no longer a being, no longer a memory, no longer a thing. There will be a day, a day of doom, that day will be the last for you to bloom. Witness the wraith that bestows upon you, you chose misery, we choose you …

"For God's sake, wake me up if it's a dream! Help!" I screamed.

Where? No idea,

Did something happen? No idea.

Chapter: 8

A haze,

Blurred horizons,

Fog everywhere.

I can see myself running, on an endless road, just me, road and the forest. It seemed someone had taken away all the colours of that world, it was all pitch black with me just running away from something.

A fright,

A misery,

Chaos all around.

I was looking here and there, perhaps looking for something, something that could calm me down, someone who could take me out. Little did I know, there wasn't a single soul there, just me and them. The cool breezes had a vibe of their own, a negative radiation of their own. I ran out of breath. My legs were tired, feet filled with cuts, body bruised till its core. It was as if this was the time when my soul would leave its body and give the authority to someone new, a new host, a new alpha.

When the blackout took over me, the only thing I remember wasn't the misery or the things that were happening to me, the harm that was caused to me, the only thing I could remember were her eyes, light brown, filled with a depth in which I would happily drown. Shining like a stone filled with mystical powers, the powers of love.

Where are those eyes?

Have I lost the connection?

Am I that far from her?

Where am I?

It was at that moment, when I witnessed many of my flashbacks, the memory lane hit hard and I was now experiencing every single bit of the past flowing through me just like clouds flow through the mountain, leaving behind scars of the past, a moist yet dark memory of a bruise which will never be gone.

I saw myself driving past with my old VW, it was a familiar road, perhaps the one where I found my sentinel or maybe the one where…

Before I could think of something and give all of this a meaning, I was already in that car driving at 120kmph, back there in the rear seat, I saw that little girl from the cellar, looking at me with her spine chilling grin. It was as if she was looking through me.

Seconds after that, she looked to the other side, I was seeing all of it in my rear view mirror, but when I saw what exactly was happening there, I found the mannequin sitting right next to me, with that faceless grin.

The car was already out of my hands now, brakes weren't working, neither was my mind. The only thing that was functioning was that part of me, the one true self that was somehow searching for her, to help him get out of this.

There weren't any hands this time,

There weren't any sensations this time,

All of it was real,

All of it was in the past.

A past that never happened,

A memory which was erased,

A timeline which was forgotten,

A wound that never healed.

Was it the end?

Or was it just the prequel to the consequences?

It was that moment then and it is this moment now, I was sitting on my bed in the way I sat in that car, the same position, the same expression and the same me, the only thing that changed was the event of occurrence.

A mist of unrealism had me in. Proving all of that as a dream again. But was it actually it?

The moment my subconscious mind came back to senses, I found Sruti coming in from the door.

"Hey Marshy! I overslept. Good morning!!" She said and smiled.

"Morning!!" I said and made a gesture of hug. She came closer and hugged me.

The hug, her smile, the way she cared about me, everything about her was like a healer to my bruised soul.

Was it the past?

Was it because she wasn't there in the past and that became the reason that she couldn't take me out of that?

I still can not answer these. Y'know when a person can't answer his own questions that's when their thoughts are the most vulnerable?

Chapter: 9

A new day,

A new page.

Mechanical fluttering of eyes, no strange feelings mixing my thoughts, no philosophical surroundings and no confused timelines, just a normal morning.

The clock said 1200 hours. It'd been days since I experienced the delight of normality. A pinch of humanity, a cold start? Eh, I can say I was hankering for this.

"Wait! this ain't my room." I muttered.

It was that moment when I started looking over the whole place and found that I was in her room and she was sitting on the floor, holding one of my hands and asleep. Her warm hands, that beautiful face, her calming presence and most importantly her.

I didn't wanna wake her up, God knows what she saw. I was looking at her, stroking the strand of hair that was in front of her, Ah! my heart pounded while doing that. The moment I placed them to the back of her ear, she woke up, her eyelids slowly opened up revealing her beautiful eyes, she was looking straight at me, the innocence in her spoke a lot about her worried thoughts.

"You okay?" I said.

"Me? You're asking that to me?" She said on a serious note.

"Whoa! Did I do something?" I said.

"Mr. Bhaumik Mohanty, you fainted when you got up in the morning, you were screaming something about a girl and a mannequin, what's the matter? Are you having those nightmares again?" She said.

"Nightmares? Had that been so easy to name, I would have flaunted with a big yes. But I'm out of words, I can't express what I felt." I said in a convincing tone as she seemed more worried than she would have been after hearing what happened.

Perhaps, the moment I saw her was the last one in my conscious state. And moments after that I fell asleep, maybe because of my mental tiredness, or maybe because of experiencing the past in a loop.

A loop; what an amazing way to describe a certain turn of events, what an amazing way to cover the reality with a silver lining.

"Umm, are you going to say something else? Or are you just gonna play with your thoughts Mister?" She said.

She was still mad at me and why won't she be. I'd fainted in front of her and was expecting her to open up.

"Uh... sorry, the same thing keeps ringing in my head dear, the same pages, the same chapters combing themselves into one dreadful flow of memories; some broken, some miseries." I said.

"It was different today though." I added.

"Different? What did you see?" She said.

"A path, maybe the one which I walked on, years ago. A destination, which I thought was my end. A loop, which I was a part of. The truth, which I was bereft of. Things I knew clashed with the things that didn't make any sense. And the things which did, weren't known to me or didn't actually exist." I said.

"I really think you should take things to the experts." She said.

"Experts? I'm not going crazy dear. But that doesn't mean you are incorrect in any way, actually I did see a psychiatrist before landing here, which was why it took me longer than I said. "Yet, they told me the same thing that anyone would say and that was to increase the dosage of sleeping pills, and stimulants. But the thing is why should I use artificial methods to fight against my thoughts and prove them wrong by just numbing them, and why not actually convincing them about their incorrectness?" I added.

"Well said, but don't ya think, the one that the docs are asking you to prefer is a better and faster way to recover and in addition to that they've the expertise in handling situations like this which in turn makes them capable enough to cure you." She said.

"Cure me? I'm neither a psychopath nor a patient of mental illness, I'm in all my senses. FYI that's what your people with expertise said." I said. "Why does everyone jump into concluding the whole thing as a hoax? I'm not playing around Muff… This thing is in me. Try getting out from the perspective of the whole world and think it by yourself, as doing the prior thing will make you no different than any other individuals who judge people by what they do and not what they think." I added.

"Listen, this is your problem, you don't put up your points, what you feel or what you think in a particular situation, you just stay silent and let the world come upon you. That's not the way things work." She said.

"See? This is what I was saying, the world's perspective… It's okay I thought it's you and I won't be needing to tell you what I think, I thought you knew what was going on in my head. Nevermind, you're right I was wrong for not standing up with my thoughts and not being open about them." I said.

"Wait! Look what you're doing, whenever we have an argument you always blame me for everything at the end. And you expect me to be different from others while you treat me in the same way as others do?" She said.

"That's not what I meant!" I said.

"Oh yeah? What was this then? … *I thought I won't be needing to tell you what I think, I thought you knew what was going on in my head* … Isn't this putting the blame on me?" She said and left the room.

Chapter: 10

Tantrums, tantrums everywhere, no place to hide, sometimes it feels like a director's override. Haha

Just kidding, throwing tantrums is a way someone expresses the fact that their inner child is interacting with you no matter the actual age of the person.

I went behind her. Out of nowhere, I heard a loud thud. Thinking that she might have slipped, I ran towards her direction. There was a room

…"Melissa Stone" It read…

Now I know, it looks like a typical place, 'the' typical place, y'know what I am trying to justify.

The manor was as good as new as the restoration project was just completed by our team, but there was something that was a bit off about that room, a thing of the past, a forgotten memory, there was a rustic old metal bed in there, one can actually picture the scene if they think of an abandoned mental asylum.

It had a whole world of its own, just like a faded memory lane, it was as if I was inside an old photograph, dusty, oiled, torn and forgotten.

The only thing that concerned me was the thud and I was really hoping she wasn't hurt which was the only reason I was in there. The room ended with another door, perhaps the exit to that room. It was a bit open and all I could see on the other side was pitch black. I went towards the door thinking that Sruti might have gone inside. She does things like this when she is mad, running away from everything to someplace isolated and then waits there for me to come over and hug her, that's how she likes to get away from pain; hugs from me. Beautiful isn't it?

The thing that was surprising was the moment when I reached the door, it slammed shut. I knocked a few times. "Sruti! I'm sorry, I really am. I know I blame you sometimes, I am really sorry for that. I say stupid things when I'm out of my mind, please Muffin, come outside, give me a hug. Muffin?" I said.

There was no answer, the only thing that was audible was a high pitched weep. The thing that felt misplaced was, I knew she never cries like this, no matter how bad the situation is, if she cries, she keeps her head on my shoulders and hugs me tight. She never weeps by herself, never at least not after we became friends.

It did seem like her voice but I knew she would never do this. "Who's it?" I said. "Who's there inside? Where's she?" I added.

The room was filled with silence,

The chilly breeze that was coming from outside, had stopped,

The sunlight started to turn black, thick dark clouds started to form up.

The thing that went unnoticed by me was the place where we were, and the place that was visible from the window of that room wasn't the same.

'Pennhurst Special Care - A house for the people who need love by the people who love.' I saw a sign which was placed outfront past the yard filled with darkness and gloom.

It was an asylum. Pennhurst Asylum to be more specific.

Wait, I have heard that name before, I have written it somewhere too. I was sure that she wasn't in here and neither should I. The moment when I started walking out, the door that had slammed shut, started opening on its own.

A squeaking noise broke the silence of the whole room, squeaking old wood, y'know how scary it sounds and all of it happening in a place where someone will highly expect to happen.

I looked back towards the door I entered through, it was still open but there was something that took my attention; the walls.

'Survive the red if you can.' It was written all over the walls. At this moment too I focussed my whole self on the point of finding her and getting out of this sequence.

'Colours demand sacrifice.' I saw it appear on one of the walls, it wasn't there at first. And the weird thing

about this situation was that the writings looked fresh which was backed up by the red fluid dripping down from the walls.

"Bhaumik!? Are you there?" I heard someone. "Sruti! I'm here!! Help!" I said. "Bhaumik? I'm sorry, I shouldn't have said that, I know you're here, Marshyy where are you?" She said.

"She can't hear you. Bhaumik. I got your name correct this time right Dr. Micheal Shultz?" Someone said.

I turned and found a girl, probably in her teens, standing next to that door. She had blood oozing out from her body, a bloodied scalpel in one of her hands and a glass bottle in another.

The moment I held the door open, she threw that large bottle.

It made contact with my hand and in moments, it shattered. I honestly didn't feel the pain at first, at all. I just felt as if something was dripping down my hand, I looked down and realized that it was severed. I was looking directly at my bone, blood was pouring. I never knew what a breakdown looks like, but seeing all of this happening in front of my eyes, it was like someone pushing me out of myself.

"Why? Why is it always me? Why me?" I weeped in pain.

"The more you resist, the more you feel, the more you avoid, the more it reveals. I warned you about the demanding nature of colours, and especially the sacrifice that is associated with red." She said with a grin and started approaching me.

"Bhaumik! What's all this?" Sruti said and rushed towards me. The moment I turned towards her, everything went back to normal again and that room which I was in was none other than my room itself.

Chapter: 11

The same dull room, yet the pastel coloured walls gave my eyes a sense of relief, starting from all the picture frames hanging and few of the cutest gifts that she once gave me when we were at college lied on the bed side table. My bed too, was unaltered. The only thing that was now weird was me being the part of two worlds, one where I lived in and the one which was a pretentious past. The only link that I had with this beautiful world was her against the numerous nightmares that stood for the later.

"Why were you talking to the wall?" she said. "I… er… uh…" "Leave the punctuation with you and please just let it be. Alright, there's nothing for you to mansplain me. Whenever I try to give you a point, you try to fit yours in to make yourself the one who faced everything on his own and the one who knows and has tried everything." She said. …*But isn't that how conversation works? Do I just keep listening and nod on everything and not even speak for myself? …* I thought. "Nope, you're right. I do make things complicated just to make my point stand out." I said.

"Oh wait, don't apologize, I guess I'm at fault. That's it. I'm sorry." She said. Though she said something, the way she said toned down to something else. "Why do you always have to do this? If you think I'm wrong, so be it. Why are you saying that so casually? Maybe try being a bit polite?" I said.

I was sobbing by then, I still don't know why I sob on things so mere but maybe its because I started expecting. It was perhaps around our first year when she started to change the way we did certain things. There was something that made her upset. The fact that people get attached to others and then somehow lose touch, few of them carry that till the end by not being able to see themselves with someone else just for the constant feeling of the past. They do forget that maybe by thinking so the one who's in the present gets to know that maybe they are wrong and a bond can never exist till death separates people. They learn it the hard way, a way that they only heard in stories of others past.

"Listen, don't get me wrong but I'm seriously mad at you and might end up saying things you don't like so it's better if you just leave the solitude to me." she said.

I couldn't make eye contact and went past her. It wasn't the first time that we argued on this, the same lines, the same words and the same thoughts. She did make sense. Everytime. I was the one who was at fault. I kept walking, I was totally taken aback by my thoughts that I forgot to watch my step.

Everything went black again, I was unconscious yet I could sense something at the back of my head. The world around me was as if it was dipped into something much darker. Rusted furniture, torn wallpapers and paint that seemed like it no one restored it for centuries.

"Every grand manor has its secrets Bhaumik." A voice whispered. "Is it you again?" I said. "Who else did you expect? I saw you were a bit gloomy so I thought you might need a friend, an acquaintance maybe?" It said. "Well, you don't lie though, that's the only thing good about you." I said. "Good? Don't associate that cursed word with me." It said. "Ever considered what people on the other side do just to be called that?" I said.

"Hmm, I think you need to stop being so 'the g word' to everyone you talk to." It said. "The g word? Seriously? Just say it. It's just the word good. You don't have to make it sound like a slang. C'mon." I said.

"So we are friends. Aren't we?" It said. "Well, you're the only one here to talk to so yeah it's like I've no other choice. "So, don't you think friends should share what they've in their minds?" It said. "My mind? Isn't it already yours?" I said. "Well, not completely. there's a part of you, a part of us that still believes in the other side. "Hold it. This is the other side, that is the real world. So I guess that gives you the answer." I said. "What is holding you back then, you know you're more powerful here, you know we all would move under you. Then why not?" It said.

"You already know who keeps me there, the reason to see beauty as it is. The reason I smile for." I said. "That reason of yours, is it here with you or is it here for you? We are always there for you but you never cherish us, the only thing you cherish is nonexistent." It said.

"Ever tried loving someone?" I said. A silence filled the void of consciousness and soon the dark clouds started to fade away.

"Bhaumik, you alright?" Deepak said while holding my head upright with everyone surrounding me. I supposedly fell down the stairs. "A trippy jump in consciousness I suppose?" I said.

They all took me to a chair and had me rested. "Hey! What happened? Sruti said while coming down in a hurry. "I'm sorry. I'm so sorry, I wasn't here. It wouldn't have happened otherwise." She started to sob. "It's okay, I was the one who pissed you off lately, don't blame it on yourself." I said.

It was still a bit hazy and I was completely uncertain of my surroundings. I was even unsure if any of this ever happened. The last thing I remember and the thing that I'm seeing now is I am with her with my head resting on her lap and her looking at me as if it was my last day here.

... I still remember what she said when we had first started going out. "I'll always hold you tight like there's no tomorrow or daylight." ...

"This moment, you and everything, is it real?" I said trying to hold my eyes up and looking right in hers. A small tear fell on my cheek. "Yes I am here with you and everything is real." She said.

I closed my eyes and smiled at her. She was here. Here with me.

"Wanna go out?" I said and got up. She was sitting there with her dress all soaked up with tears. I hugged her tight and whispered, "Let me be your fantasy" She was singing the lines of an old rhyme that I made for her she did sing till this point and waited for me to wake and tell her that, little did she know I was there with her all the time just wanting to be with her and live in that moment for as long as it was possible.

She sobbed more and hugged back tight. I stood up and she clinged on to me just like a small baby. "Hey, it's alright, I'm here na?" I said. "C'mon, I have a surprise for you." I said. She was not at all in the mood to even look down at me; she was just there holding me tight.

She did come down when I almost took her in that state down the hall, but she held my hands as if it were a kid afraid of losing out. We went out.

I blindfolded her as it was a planned surprise. She likes surprises. We drove for 18 km and finally we reached our destination. She was acting like a child and was holding my hand too tight out of excitement. "Okayyy, okayy you can open that now, my god look at this kid." I said.

No sooner than she opened the blindfold, I could see her eyes tearing up. I actually had completely recreated a moment from our past. Our first concert together. The same stage, the same singer and the same season. I had it all planned way back when I wasn't even here. I wanted her to feel like we were still there. Just where we started. I also gave her a book which I had preserved for ages. Every page was with a flower that she gave me.

"For us" I said.

She was smiling at me and we locked our eyes for quite a while. "You.. you are… you are mine." She said. "I know that. Do you?" I said.

Chapter: 12

Warmth,

A word that is known to everyone,

Yet no one relates to,

A feeling that everyone aspires,

Yet there are few who make it through.

…

Y'know when you open your eyes next to a person whom you had cherished all your life, a person who sure was unsure about what to expect from the nearing events that she almost forgot. Sometimes it is better to focus more on moments than memories.

Yet with all that chaos, she did make it through. Not alone but with a moment, she never accepted it but always had it.

There she was right next to me, holding my little finger with hers. I woke up next to her. That same innocent face, the same strand of her hair covering her eyes, painting her with all the hues of joyous love and serenity.

I extended my hand to feel her face, rubbed my thumb against her soft cheeks. Y'know when there's a phase when you want time to stop there and expect nothing else.

Sooner I noticed her eyes, they started to move, struggling between her dreamland and the real world. "Hey sleepyhead..." I said. "It's dawn already?" She said, rubbing her eyes.

We could hear distant chirrups, rays of the sun slowly started getting through the curtains with a certainty to wake two more birds. Haha.

"It's not even breakfast time yet. Stop thinking na..." she said in a sweet voice. "I wasn't thinking, I was ..." "yeah, yeah, bleh blah blah... stop that." She said and reached up and pulled me down to her, and the rest of my thoughts were lost against her mouth. I kissed her gently with a bliss, yet it wasn't gentleness she wanted, not now, not after all this time, and she knotted her fists in mine, pulling me against her. My arms circled her, gathering her against me, and we rolled over, still kissing.

Before she could withdraw her mind from its far places, my arms were around her, as sure and hard. She felt again the rush of helplessness, the sinking yielding, the surging tide of warmth that left her limp. And the quiet face of hers was blurred and drowned to nothingness. I bent back her head across my arm and kissed her, gentler again, and then with a swift gradation of intensity that made her cling to me as the only solid thing in a dizzy swaying world. My insistent mouth were parting her shaking lips, sending wild tremors along her nerves, evoking from her sensations she had never known she was capable of feeling. And before a swimming giddiness spun her round and round, she knew that she was kissing me back.

We laughed, we giggled, we did enjoy the way everything turned into. An adventure that no one plans yet is deluded by all.

Me made out? Umm... we could if she would have been less ticklish. Uh... yeah you get it. So let's not go there as I couldn't. Haha. Kidding.

"Ugh, c'mon sorry. Come back here!" She said. "You have no right to say that, get up, we have work to do." I said. "Don't be mad at me, you know I'm a bit ticklish." She said. "Bit? Really? Haha, very funny" I said.

Someone knocked on the door. "Yeah?" I said. There was no reply.

"Get ready, I'll just check what's going on outside." I said. "No. Wait, we'll go together, just give me some time, I'll be ready in five." She said and went into the bath.

Her five actually meant thirty-five. "Seriously Muff?" I said. "Hihi, let's gooo" she said. She held my hand and pulled me out. Not an inch. "Haha, ever considered your weight?" I said and laughed. I went forward and took her out, she was so pissed off.

These little fights, these little inconveniences, aren't these what makes us strong? I do think and believe it.

"See? Everyone's ready and all freshened up.

And your slow coach always has to take more than five minutes just getting a shirt on." She said. "Me? Ahaan? Okay... that's exactly what happened." I said.

The whole team was ready, we had new research to carry forward.

... I think I need to say a bit more on what we do. Our team restores vintage mansions and sites and converts it to a sustainable livable space.

Yeah, seems boring? It's not. Imagine having to analyse abandoned buildings and trying to carve beauty out of it.

It was the best of moments, it was the worst of memories, it was the beauty of old quotes, it was the curse of new chapters, it was the spring of hope, it was a winter of despair, as one of those sides was a gruesome liar.

The trees had started to wave back with their leaves while sprinting against us. It was an hour drive yet a beautiful one.

"It's always the path not the destination" she said and held my hand while I changed the gear. I didn't say anything neither did she. We took a glance at each other and started to feel us with the wind as if we were mere leaves floating in air.

Light and calm.

No we weren't seasons.

We were us.

Chapter: 13

You can forever be older than you ever knew yourself but can never get rid of parts of you that stayed there.

A part from us,

A part that felt heavy when it came through,

A part that we could never hold on to.

A lil' no worth,

A precious phase.

…

Cold bricks

The building was tan stucco and wood slat, built around grassy knolls.

I stared up at the arch, knowing little of the history, only the name. It was yet another symbol of a glorious empire that had collapsed into the dust of this desolate place.

What armies have you seen? I thought. How many generals have passed beneath you, expecting their accomplishments to stand like this, a monument to history?

I stood there with the old mansion that once was a home to a writer of some sort. That is what the locals said.

"Must be a place with a lot of secrets." Deepak said. All of us stood there looking at the wilderness it had pondered upon. All of the front was taken over by whites. "Aren't these beautiful?" She said. "Uh-uh! don't touch that." I said and pulled her back. "These are purple hyacinths. They're always attached to the ones who are in sorrow." I added.

"Hey, it's okay, hold your horses. Just flowers… alright? No need to make things up." Deepak said. "Yeah, you're right I'm thinking a bit too loud these days." I said "Now come on, let's get in." He added.

The ivy crawled up the sides of the building, and the windows were boarded up, giving it a sense of abandonment. Despite its decay, the mansion had an eerie vibe to it. The broken panels shouted the weight of its history and the secrets it held. Somewhere within, I hesitated, but my zeal to research got the best of me. We pushed open the creaky door to explore the forgotten mansion.

Desperation can drive away things that were meant to be yet, the ones willing to hold them in can make it through. The four of us stood next to an elite masterpiece that faced the ravages of time. Composed mostly of gilt and glass, the mansion showed the essence of Baroque.

This sure was way older than we expected. The rooms were prodigious. "Hey look!" Auromic pointed at a painting on top of a fireplace. "Looks like someone got time to paint the mansion in its prime." He said. "Looking at the craftsmanship, it aged really well." Sruti added.

It had once been a grand estate, but now it was worn down by time and neglect.

"But why will anyone want this beauty to rust out?" Deepak said. "Well, it's always better for things to rust out than wear out." I replied. "Cheers to that, but that added up a lot of hassle for us to restore. No matter how great the previous owner was, it is on us how we create it for the next one." He added.

We pressed on, it was not only enormous from the outside but the interior reflected it too. Our footsteps echoed through the empty halls.

Every corner seemed to hold a new surprise, as if the mansion was alive and taunting us. "Doesn't it feel a bit.. umm what's the word…" Deepak was about to finish when I said, "Eerie? well it's an old mansion, this is the least we can expect from it. Dear trying to be a spooky mansion, you hold higher standards." I said

As they explored deeper into the mansion, we found ourselves in a grand ballroom that was somehow still standing despite the decay of the rest of the mansion. The room was filled with cobwebs, but the chandelier still glimmered with a faint light. "Seriously? A ball room and that to be in a writer's house? Sruti said. "Well, It wasn't always like this. It used to be a living room which was later converted into this." I said. "Uh-huh… wait, how do you know that?" She said. "I just do." I said. "Dude, are you on pills again?" Auromic said. "What pills?" I said. "Wait, why does it seem like a déjà vu?" He added. "I don't know man. Let's just stick to the research." I said and headed towards the stairs.

Regardless of everything, my thoughts were still wandering on the possibilities of the familiarity of this place.

How do I know what this place was and most importantly why?

The moment I approached the staircase, I felt flashes of memories, the ones that were blurred with time. "You okay?" She said. "You seem a bit lost." She added. "I feel a bit nauseous but I would say I'm finding myself within these hallways." I said. "Marshy, I think you should step out for some fresh air." She said and held me in. "No, wait look, if I'm not wrong, you'll find a small window by the stairs, near to the next floor, there's a door too. A smaller one next to it would be just at the landing level with frames in between the both" I said holding both of us back.

"Listen sweetheart, you're just tired. But yeah I'll look up for that window, just so you get your mind cleared up." She said and took a few steps up and stopped right after taking another step. She gave me a look of confusion yet fright.

I followed her to find two windows that preceded a

door to a room. The same way I explained it to her. "But how?" She said. "Just like I said. I just do. It's my first visit to this place, rather, the first one in this state. Yet I have blurred memories, which tell me that I know something that I surely have forgotten. Or maybe it didn't happen to me but a feeling that wants me to take it in." I said.

"Hey you guys! Anything up?" Deepak said. "Umm yeah there's a room in here, probably locked." I said. Sruti was still staring at me.

I knew how she felt, as once I was there too. Or maybe here too.

"Well, gonna crank that up." He said and headed towards the door. Even after consecutive tries and with a lot of change of tools, the door stood erect. "Not even a scratch?" Auromic said. "Perhaps just a prop, let's not waste more time on this and head back to the manor." I said.

It was not just me being logical for it, it was also because of the fright that something might happen to them.

As soon as everyone got off the last stair, I looked back for one last time. The door had changed into a familiar one, perhaps from my childhood, it was a bit open. I could clearly sense someone looking at me straight into my eyes as if I was the one invading something that was meant to be for someone else. It slowly closed back to the way it was before.

"I don't feel good here. Can we head back home?" Sruti said. She was waiting for me at the landing, I didn't notice her, but I think she did for what I felt. "Yea.. Yeah let's leave." I said and rushed down to her. I gave her a side hug and held her hands in mine. "There's nothing to be afraid of. It's just something…." Before I could complete, she held me firmly and I could sense that all of it happening to me caused a bit of discomfort to her.

I said nothing thereafter, just held her and we went back to our car. I got the car running and turned it back to the manor.

"It has been getting windy lately. Right muff?" I said. She didn't say a word. Just held my hand firmly and kept looking at me all emotional. "Heyy, it's okay, I am okayy." I said and rubbed her shoulder a bit. "Don't worry we'll get back in no time." I said and accelerated the car.

It was around a kilometer or two before we reached, and it started to pour. The wet soil and the sound of the drops took away all the pain and worries. Y'know, when you enjoy the spills, you know nothing can heal you better than this.

We reached the manor after a couple of misdirections that I purposefully took to enjoy the weather. She too was a bit happy after it rained. I could finally see her beautiful eyes blinking softly. Just like a petal falling smoothly down with the winds, her eyes beautifully whispered something about a good ol' nap.

"Hey sleepy head, wake up, we reached home." I said by gently brushing my hand against her cheeks. She opened her eyes, her innocent looks were more than enough to make me forget about the greatest regrets, oh my sweet hazel.

We got back in, I switched on the lamp and made her rest on the bed by the headboard. "Carolina, wait up here I'll make you some hot chocolate." I said and gave her a forehead kiss. She blinked at me twice with her cute eyes.

"Here's the room service. A special hot chocolate for a special someone." I said and gave her a cup. She smiled at me and took a few sips. "Yummyyy!" She said. The moment I turned back for my cup and turned towards her again, she was already asleep.

Uff...

I sat next to her and covered her with a blanket.

Rainy nights,

Smell of wet soil,

Cold breezes,

A person to adore upon.

I took a sip to toast on how lucky I was.

Chapter: 14

My watch chimed again, yep, I am old school, I still use the hourly chime settings in my watch. It's better to know if the time was just as slow as my retrospection that keeps kicking in from time to time. It was already quarter past three at night. There was still some hot chocolate left in my mug. It was as if I froze in time. I took the last sip, regardless of the fact that it'd been two hours since I made it.

Well, it's hot chocolate. I mean now it's cold… Umm… Who cares? Haha.

I got up and went to the window, my favourite place. I sat by the side of it. It's that feeling y'know, when everyone's asleep, you open the louvres and look at the beautiful world from a little opening, the one which connects your lil' world with that of others.

A peaceful existence,

The one with solitude yet camaraderie,

The one which is transient yet perennial,

A beautiful one.

She was sleeping, unaware of the outer world, unaware of everything that was going on. Just like a child who knows nothing except the things that are in her reach. Young, sweet and silly. I sighed to my thoughts.

I sat there looking at her and the world outside, ain't this love?

I smiled to myself and looked at the moon, it had stopped raining but the beauty of nature never fades with time or season. Our lives are transient in front of the infinite love given by nature.

My phone chimed. There was some notification.

... Hey Bhaumik!

Wait, who could possibly text me this late at night? I ignored it thinking it was supposedly a prank.

... Hey dude, stop ignoring, I know you're up man. It read.

... Hi there! Who's this? I texted.

... Seriously? you haven't saved my number? What sorta brother are you? It read.

... It's Savv, how're things going? It's been a while and you haven't texted. So I thought you'd be 'busy'.... She texted.

... Uh-oh! Hehe... sorry dude, I was actually a bit preoccupied with work and stuff. Well, everything is great here, being with her heals me just as it did in college. I texted back.

… Ohh, it's alright, I am happy that you could move on from being trapped in your own thoughts. I'm glad that finally you two are there together. Did you ask her out yet? She texted.

… I was going to but there are things which are taking a turn. I texted.

… What do you mean 'are taking a turn'? She replied.

… I think my mind is playing games again… I saw something ridiculous today at work. You see? The more I try to get these things out of my head, the more they try to crawl back in. I texted.

… Oh… okayy, that's not good, did you tell her that? She replied.

… Tell? She saw that for herself and I think she isn't ready to handle those yet, she's seeing me suffer the way no one has. It is obvious that she would be terrified when she sees what I have gone through. That is exactly the reason stopping me. I texted.

… You love her. That's for sure. It's quite late anyway. Now go get some rest. And yeah ask her out, c'mon I am getting old, at least I wanna enjoy some cringey songs when you guys tie a knot. She texted.

… Woah, easy there. Haha. See ya. I replied and turned my phone off.

All of it was real, the love, the charm, the calmness everything. The only thing that was making me think twice was the thing I saw back there. I wasn't sure of what it was but I could tell that the thing that occurred there was somehow related to me, it was like a memory that I had forgotten.

A thing of the past, I wasn't sure if it was from my past, as if I was unaware of my own existence in that memory. The harder I tried to think of it, the farther it was from me. It was as if there was something that was masking it from me, someone had something to do with all this.

I usually don't forget things but this was one of those things which I never did but the memory of me experiencing it was far more real than the excuse that my mind kept giving to itself to calm me down.

I closed my eyes to recapitulate what had happened. Isn't it quite obvious that when we close our eyes, there's just our consciousness within infinite darkness? But this wasn't the case this time. The moment I closed my eyes, I found myself in a bed, way different than where I was supposed to be. To my surprise, it wasn't any type of varied consciousness, it was just me and I was sure of it because when I opened my eyes, I found myself in my own bed but the moment I closed them, I was back in that room. Well it could be called a perspective of nothingness, where I was trapped.

Curiosity kills the cat. And that always gets me in trouble. I wanted to know more about it. So I purposefully closed them and wandered upon the visions of someone else's memory. The more I tried, the more I came to know that it was difficult to control it. It was me but I couldn't control it. It was as if everything was like a cutscene. A playable character that was in tutorial mode.

…Yeah, I know, teenage stuff. But I'm almost out of it. Don't judge me for that… haha… Let's get back to it…

It was a dark room with just the amount of light to see where things were near me. It was a pretty old room with a seeped out wallpaper on the walls. A door to my right which was supposedly closed from inside. I was looking around to see if I knew this place and something about it was a bit off yet seemed familiar to me as if I grew old here. The sky was dark and covered with clouds as if it was about to rain soon. The cracked up windows showed that the room and perhaps the house did belong to a noble man who went bankrupt. I saw myself in the mirror, It was hazy yet I could figure out that I was way younger than I was supposed to be. I was seeing myself and before I could analyze what was actually happening, I heard someone at the door, trying to open it.

"Shh! don't make any noise, he is back again for you." Someone said. I saw that something was hiding beneath the bed. "Get down here son." It said again. It was female, at least from her voice. It started with a rough pull at the knob and then all of it ended with banging the door, perhaps with tools, someone was trying to break into that room.

After consecutive failed attempts, it did manage to break through but when the door knob actually broke, I heard footsteps receding down the stairs. The moment everything was calm, she came out from the space beneath and struggled standing, supposedly because of age. It sure was a horrific scene to witness as she was no doubt a human but her skin was stuck down to her bones, It was like a single epidermal layer above the skin. No eyes, as if her soul was long gone.

"Who was it?" I said.

"Shhh… don't ask anything yet. I'll ring you once dinner is served." She said and went out.

I was still there trying to get hold of what just happened. I saw the walls of the room, they were scribbled all around as if a child took the walls as his canvas. There was a specific one that took my attention. It was a child with a person, perhaps his mother and that child was supposedly the one I was.

Soon I heard a bell ringing at a distance. Thinking it was a call for dinner, I stood up and approached the door. The moment I opened it, I saw a man, looking straight at the door right on the landing.

It was me! The real me, who kept walking down after we shared a glance. I was right about this. The thing that I saw there was something that was connected to me somehow and it sure was trying to say something.

The moment I walked down, the scene started getting blurry, as if my presence in that mansion made everything connect and when I went out the connection was broken.

I opened my eyes to my real self, still by the side of the bed, sitting near the window with everything that I loved being unaltered.

Chapter: 15

My sleepy eyes opened to a sense of numbness. The sun did rise again but the warmth to my soul was holding me tight. She was hugging me tight, her head resting on my arm and her face snuggled within. "Wakie… wakie." I said and brushed my finger on her nose. She shook her head and turned her face to the other side.

Ahh… these lil' things. It's always these lil' things that make me fall for her.

"Hey, you know what? Let's go somewhere today." I said. "Wh… where?" She said in a drowsy voice. "C'mon, not everything special has to have a destination right? It can also be the journey." I said. "I just woke up Marsh… Don't hit me with those complex bleh bleh blah of yours." She said. "Hehe. Get up sweetie, you'll see." I said. "No! Lemme sleep na?" She said.

I gave her an expressionless face. "Okayy… okayy, I'm getting up. Now get rid of that face please." She said. "Good girl." I said with a smile. "Now get ready for some old school hangout." I added. "Old school eh? Hmm…

Mister, I would like you to step out of this room" She said. "Is that necessary?" I said with a grin. "Ahhaan. It sure is. Now the exit is that way." She said and pointed to the door. "Okay… okayy… I almost forgot that you never made me giddy up." I said with a wry smile and left the scene.

Just as usual, I was ready within minutes yet someone was still setting up their curler. How do I know? Experience.

"All set! Let's go!" She said after being in the room for the past hour. "Yes your majesty." I said. "Oh c'mon, I was quick this time." she said. "That's what she said." I said and grinned. "You're disgusting y'know that right?" She said with sass. "Yep, I know. Now let's get going." I said.

I took her, arm in arm, to my car and opened the door for her. Gentleman you suppose? Ahem, that's called protecting your car from slamming your doors. Haha. I hope she doesn't know.

I got in and kissed her on the forehead. "Hehe. Where are we going? You didn't mention that." She said and blushed.

"I don't know. Yet." I replied with a grin. "Let's just see where the car takes us." I added. "You're driving it. So you know it." She said. "I meant where the road takes us." I added and laughed.

We were filling up our love with our presence. As we drove, the sun casted a warm glow over the rolling hills around us. The hours passed quickly, and before we knew it, the sun was beginning to set.

"Look at the colors." she said looking at the sky that turned first orange, pink, and then purple. "It's like a painting." She added.

"I know," I said, glancing over at her. "It's beautiful." I added.

"What is?" She said and started to swirl her strands of hair. "Well, the view definitely." I said and laughed. "Yeah. Fine. The view. Why not?" She said grumpily. "You're my best view. My lil' Hazel." I said and squeezed her cheeks. She tried controlling her smile but I noticed it.

We drove in silence for a while, the only sounds coming from the radio and the soft rustle of leaves in the breeze. Finally, we reached a lookout point with a breathtaking view.

"Wow!" she whispered as we parked the car and stepped out. "This is amazing." She added.

We stood there for a while, arm in arm, lost in the beauty of the moment and the overwhelming feeling of being together.

"I'm so glad we did this." she said, leaning into me.

"Me too." I replied, kissing the top of her head.

As we stood there, wrapped up in the magic of the moment, I could sense that she didn't want to go back home just yet.

"What do you say, we stay out a little longer?" I said hoping she would agree. She looked up at me. "Yes! Yes! yess!" she said, taking my hand.

We got back into the car and continued driving, the night breezes rushing through the open windows. We drove for what felt like hours, talking and laughing as the miles slipped by.

Finally, we pulled over, surrounded by fields of swaying grass. We got out of the car and lay down on the hood, gazing up at the stars above us.

"This is perfect." she said, snuggling into my side.

I couldn't agree more. As we lay there, wrapped up in each other's arms, I knew that this was a moment that would stay with us forever.

As the hours slipped by, we watched the stars slowly begin to fade as the sun started to rise. It was a bittersweet moment, knowing that our adventure was coming to an end.

But as we drove back home, I knew that this was only the beginning of our journey together.

Chapter: 16

Days went by and our team did manage to pull up with the research on that mansion. The field work and the analysis was done with all the details down to the last bit.

"So, finally we're done with all the literature study and preliminary concepts." I said. We had thought to give it the same old Baroque vibe. Just with a pinch of modernity. "So, you're saying we can start off with the designs?" Sruti said. "Perhaps." I said. "Umm... Bhaumik, man we need one more thing for it. Just one." Deepak said. "Shoot." I said. "We need to know a concrete history of the mansion, the 'writer' thing is getting tilted towards the rumor side.

"Ah... that's true. Well, that leaves me to get back to the eerie." I said with a mediocre face. "Hehe. We have to because we need it." Auromic said. "Okayy, okayy, I didn't deny it. Did I?" I said and got up. Before I could reach the keys... "Hey! Forgetting something?" She said with squinched eyes. "You don't have to. Sweetheart, it's just some minor deets. I can handle it." I said. "You're saying, I would allow you. You, the person who vanished from my life for more than half a decade, are going to go somewhere without me? Seriously?" She said and grabbed the keys and marched forward towards the car.

What? You think I was gonna do something? Obviously not, I was the one at fault. Can't argue on that.

"You're driving? Seriously? Don't kill us." I said and laughed.

"Haha, rest in peace mister." She said with a grin. It took her a few trial starts to just put it in motion. Women.

We drove off, a bit rough yet enjoyable. Eh we'll be fine right? Right?

"You really are thinking if we'll make it safe. Isn't it?" She said. "Na..ah nothing like that sweetie." I said. "Can say from the sweating." She said with a smirk. "Don't worry. Dude chill." She added.

It seemed convincing. Yet the experience flashed before me. She once crashed us with a tree trunk. None of us was injured though. It all happened as someone wanted to try a no hand drive on a freeway. Yep. That's always someone with a crazy ambition.

We were minutes away from the mansion when we saw the weather taking turns for a good shower. It wasn't until we reached, when we saw a tint of sepia all over the place surrounding the mansion.

"Why is it always the yellows?" She said. "Maybe someone had to paint the world in a way they see their memories." I said with a sigh. "Are you trying to say that someone's writing all of this? And we are just the characters?" She said with amusement. "Maybe it's not exactly written, but maybe it is fate that people misunderstand as a decision." I said.

By that time, she had put the car in park. "You really had to. No, can't you just be a bit normal while talking about things, do you always have to be philosophical?" She said with irritation. I laughed it off and got out of the car.

It still had its rustic charisma filling the surrounding with a lucrative essence. "It doesn't fail to grab attention even in these tones of the sky." she said. "Some things live to last and some last to live. But yeah it kinda shouts eerie in every language." I said. "That is for sure but the legacy it holds is what matters to us. She said.

"Oh look, the flowers!" She exclaimed. "Weren't they different the other day?" I said. "It's okay the previous owner must have planted seasonal ones, one dies and the other blooms." She said.

Sometimes, flowers teach a lot about life. May it be a lily that signifies elegance and shows how delicate is beauty to us humans and then there's dahlia, that prospers even when the crowd fails to, signifying the dominance of self in life with solitude. Nature is what defines how we act with our decisions and how the decisions are connected with consequences.

Sruti was always fascinated with flowers. No matter the colour or fragrance, every flower was her friend and she enjoyed their company. "Look, there's a lot more over there." She said. I smiled at her and said, "When the beauty of nature met the beauty of creation."

I let her be in her world of colours and let myself in through the doorway of the mansion. Being wrapped in the theme of Baroque, the glare inside made it feel like the golden hour. Everything shined as good as new, just like it froze in time after the residents abandoned it. To my surprise, there were certain changes that I felt compared to the day we came in.

The rooms weren't the way they were on that day, they were oriented in a different way as if someone reverted back to where it came from. It was slightly more like the version I somehow remembered from a forgotten memory.

The rooms, the living space, the atriums, everything was just like it used to be. I was surprised to see it as the thing I thought was a memory, was actually a prediction. Or maybe this place, this time, everything in it, went back in time and froze just for me to witness.

The wallpapers, the paintings and even the sculptures seemed new. As if I came in just after it opened for being used.

A mansion in its full glory,

A mansion in a way we saw.

… Is it just me or is it actually in a time paradox?

… Is it the past that is repeating itself to show the hearty and beautiful ambiance it created many years ago or is it the final design that we would come up with after a few years?

… What was this all about?

These were the uncertainties that were randling around in my head.

The first thing that made me anxious was the room. I ran upstairs to see for myself, whether the thing I saw that night was actually a part of reality or was it the masked version of it.

Chapter: 17

As soon as I reached the floor above, I saw an open door. The room that was once difficult to break in, was now shining in the sun like a pearl upon the ocean, with its gleaming wallpapers and ornate furniture.

The windows were beautifully painted with whites and tones, I could also see Sruti still enjoying herself in the flowerbed. We waved at each other and exchanged smiles. I saw everything, the things that were torn once, seemed as if they were recrafted in their exact structures just the day before. It was even in the walls, the paint seemed fresh too.

It was quite an astonishing view yet was terrifying at the same time. The same room which was giving a sense of being born again just a while ago, turned into a massacre of a mistake. I found a few polaroids in the corner that were familiar to one of my nightmares that I used to have a few years ago. Not only that, there were things that were specific to me but were in the past yet managed to show up in that room. The chills ran down my spine when I also found a matte black VW Beetle left completely totaled in the garage.

I ran outside out of fright. "The... there... there's the car." I said fumbling and sweating. "Hey, calm down a bit. You seem a bit too flustered right now." She said and hugged me. It's always that one person who tends to take away all your fears with just a simple hug.

"Now tell me what happened." she said. "There's a lot of thin... things there. I... It seems as if I was the one living in it at some point of time. Yet there's nothing that I can remember of. Everything is connected to something yet nothing makes sense to make it a part of something." I said. "It's okay, let's just see what the house has for us." she said and insisted on getting in. "No... I don't think we should." I said but before I could say anything else, she sealed me with a kiss. "Now, let's go." she said and pulled me in.

No, there's no pun intended, I literally went in. Haha. I meant the house.

The things now were very different. It was the same old mansion, with all the creepers and peeled off wallpapers. The rusted interiors yelled their centuries in service. The rooms oriented in the same way as we saw on that very day.

"Ho... How is this possible?" I mumbled. "They were right. I swear, I saw..." I said. "Shh... Marshy, I know you saw something and I do believe in you. Let's see if we find something that relates to what happened and what's happening." She said and took my hand.

"Thank you for that, I thought you would say I made it all up." I said. "What? You do remember, we know each other from college right? And I do know, you won't lie to me on something this serious." she said. I smiled and said, "This way, let's see if we find something up stairs." I said and led the way to the upper floor.

Even though the mansion reverted back to the way it was before, the room up the stairs was still the same. It was as if someone forgot to take everything back. It seemed like a glitch in the altering.

"Oh look! The room is open!" She exclaimed. "I guess I wasn't all wrong and it wasn't just happening in my mind." I said and gasped. "Hey you don't need to prove anything, now tell me what you saw inside." She said. "There was once a time when I had visions, I preferred calling them nightmares as they were too eerie and realistic to just be a part of someone being asleep." I said. "Once I saw something that made me think twice about everything as I woke up to the same place where it all started but I was never asleep. Of all the things I had gone through on that day, there was one blurred memory, a memory of a room. A room exactly like this, which also relates to a similar incident that also was connected to this room." I said.

"Whoa! wait up. You did see something like that yet you didn't think of mentioning it to me?" She said. "Umm, well it was all too fast for me to hold on to that I almost forgot to tell you about it." I said. "You're ridiculous, you know that right?" she said. "Tell me about it. Now at least?" she added.

I told her everything about the kid and his mother and what exactly happened that night after we had hot chocolate together. "You think this might have something to do with you and this house?" She said. "Yes, I suppose." I said. "But as per the rumours, the previous owner was a writer and I don't think a writer would somehow try to connect to me and even if they do, they won't come to me as the way I just portrayed before you." I said. "Well, do you think it has something related to the intellect between you two?" She said.

To be very honest, having a similar mind is just as possible as finding a marble in a box of hot sand. Easier in thoughts yet difficult to make it through. The fact that I didn't put any of it as a perspective, made me retrospect more on myself.

"It might be a case of similar thinking and since you both connect on the base of the power of your thoughts, you could see what the walls saw them write." she said.

"I could feel what the notes got stained for. I could be just more than being myself for a while, as if I was them for a while." I said.

"Exactly!" She exclaimed.

"Preferences maybe? There's a thing called cognitive bias. It is a tendency of a human brain to process information from personal preferences, Or may it be the consensus effect? Where a person sees their own preferred versions of seeing things, disregarding what others see or feel." I said.

"You definitely should have taken human psychology as your major. You would have nailed it." She said. "A psycho as a psychiatrist? Seriously?" I said and laughed. "Every single one of them is like that. There's no difference you know." She said with a smirk.

"Okay now, I think that's enough information we needed for that thing. The person who lived here had some similar interests like mine but how does it define them having a car that I had during my past years? And that to be they met with an accident just like I did and did manage to get the same number plate on it?" I said.

"Wait. What?" She said and looked straight at me. "You met with an accident and totaled your car? And you never mentioned that in your emails? Seriously?" She added.

"Uhh…" Before I could complete, she said, "No! do not 'uhh' me you mister! You are in big trouble." She said. It was a few moments after that, she looked at me and said, "Why did you not tell me about it? What happened? You did recover well na? She said. "Hey, it was a minor accident, and I didn't get myself into something big, I was discharged in a couple of days." I said. I noticed her all teared up. "Hey, I am alright. Don't worry, I am in front of you right now. See? All good." I said and brushed my hands on her shoulder. "You… ann… I can't even get mad at you. Don't you think there's a person waiting for you? Can't you be more cautious while driving?" She said. "I love you, can't you get that right?" She added. "Just don't be dead. Please. Do that for me." She added again.

I stood there seeing her cheeks changing from pale to red yet her eyes were filled with emotions of a person who somehow thought she might have lost me way back when we were not even close to each other. I smiled and let her childishness take over.

"Why are you smiling? It is not funny!" she said with a puppy face. "Aww, come here." I said and extended my arms. "Nah-ah…" She said and faced the other way. "Ah… okay…" I said and started to walk the other way. "Annn, you're so mean!" she walked along my footsteps and gave me a few tender punches. Yeah she does that just to show that I'm pissing her off. I held her fist and pulled her close to a tight hug.

"I'm here for you. Don't worry about me. You're here to protect me. Aren't ya?" I said and gave her a pat on the head.

"Yes I am. Which is why you should never go out of my sight. Just stay within the closest range." She said and tried pulling my hand in hers. "Since when were you incharge of taking us? You Miss. Tender hands." I said and took her instead. She threw an expressionless face which I was sure of seeing anyway. Haha.

Chapter: 18

"Whatever, now tell me more about the car?" She said. "Uh, well here it is. You're seeing this right?" I said and pointed to the car that was smashed down to its last bits standing in the garage of that old mansion. "Holy cow! That's the car? I mean, Is that a car?" She said with astonishment.

"Umm, yeah pretty much it." I said and was ready for...

"You're saying this was your car after the accident?" She said. "Ah... no it was already my car before the accident." I said. "Shut up! You're saying, you met with a minor accident that out of nowhere smashed the car into a sheet of metal?" She said furiously. "Umm." I said. "Na-ah... ah... you are not gonna say anything right now!" She said. "You know what you mean to me right? Can't you just drive carefully?" She said. "What would have I done if something did ... di.. did happen... t.. to you?" She said and started sobbing. "It's... ahh.. umm.. I'm sorry, hey... my lil' Hazel, I'm sorry. I would never get my hands off the steering. I promise. I'll drive cautiously." I said. "You won't drive again. Promise me?" she said with her tears rolling down her cheeks.

"Sweetheart, you know that's not possible, here, come here Muff." I said and held her in a close hug. "You're bad." she said. "Haha, am I?" I said. "I should leave then? You shouldn't be around bad people." I said and pushed myself away for a while. "Ann…" she said and was about to cry. "Hey.. hey… I'm just kidding, heyy." I said to console her. "Now, wipe them off and let's see what more secrets this mansion has for us." I said. "C'mon, Hazel, it's not the kind of place we can hang around." I said and took her with me.

She made a face which was filled with a mixture of emotions. Angry, emotional yet adorable. I tried not to look at her as I wasn't acquainted with her being upset and it wasn't even the right space to cheer her up. We stood in between all the eerie and mysteriosity.

Now, where were we?

Yeah, the car. It was the same VW I used to drive around years ago and the one which the company exchanged with my Mazda. And the reason I don't believe that it is a coincidence is the number plate that this car has is registered under me. How can it be possible that a car that broke down years ago, meets me back again in the same condition after all this time.

"So, you're saying that your insurance company took this car and placed it here? That makes no sense." She said. "Umm, it won't as that might not have been what actually happened. We need to see how things got this complicated." I said and started getting towards the car.

Everything in it was just the way I left it. It was a matter of surprise tha the smiling monk on my dash was still intact. I was just seeing it for a while when Sruti said, "Oh my goodness, you still had it?" She exclaimed. "Yes, I did, and you don't know how much I tried to get it back. It was then when they said they scrapped this off. All these years and it still stands." I said and pulled it out.

It seemed as if someone kept it unhindered for me to take it back. Well, I got something that had created a void for too long. It was a showpiece that she bought for me when I was sick. She said, after I have this, I'll be happy just like the smiling monk.

"Now that's like a good friend." She said. "Yeah, sure, friend, why not?" I said and went back in to see for something. "Oh c'mon, I was just messing with you." she said and brushed my cheeks with her thumb.

"Hey look, the newspaper." I said and took it out from the glovebox. 'A car crash in the middle of a freeway, one injured' It read. There were more in there. A complete stack from the day the accident occurred, till the day I was released from the hospital. "Someone was keeping track of me." I said. "But why? I don't think you did something that nosey to have your own stalker? Or did you?" She said.

"No, it wasn't from my side, there was something that held me back from knowing what's bitter in the sweetened lies." I said and was about to get out of the door when I saw something in the rearview mirror. A face that I could never forget. Sruti was standing behind the car looking right at me. She was all teared up and was about to break down. "Hey, hey… sweetheart, what's the matter?" I said and got back to her. "It's nothing, I just imagined you driving it when this all happened." She said and started sobbing again. "Okay, wait let's get back home, have some iced americano and spend some time thinking that we are thankful to the one who made it possible. Who made 'us' possible." I said and started to head towards the car with her wiping her tears.

I took one last look at the mansion. It was all fragmented and nothing actually made any sense. The only thing that made it to reality was the old mansion which stood there, stuck in time with all its mysteries worth the entire lifetime.

The dusk settled in,

The world changed from being in dull yellow, to tints of orange and pink,

It was worth everything,

A place where one could be happy, sad and confused at the same time,

A place, where one felt lighter even in the middle of chaos,

A place, where one would lose all his hopes on and then gain it all back,

A place called home,

Her.

Chapter: 19

"Hey, you guys alright?" Deepak said with a pat on my shoulder. "Uh… yeah, we are. Why are you asking all of a sudden?" I said. "You were gone for the whole day, and God knows when you came back. We were worried for you two." He said. "Whole day? As far as I remember, it was dusk when we came back from the mansion." I said. "Umm, no, there's all of us who will definitely oppose it. We did give you both a call yet none of your cells were reachable." He said.

"Whoa! Okay, that seems a bit delusional." I said. "It might. But how come it took you so long, you were there for history ain't it?" He said. "And how on earth are you asleep on the porch of a manor with a lady? Do you even have any idea how dangerous it is?" He added.

I was still drowsy, yet I managed to open my eyes to the golden hour of the day. Cutting across the canopies with mild breezes. It was strange yet beautiful. Both of us were at the porch of the manor with her by my side, clinging to my arm.

The car was right in front and we supposedly were

so tired that we slept then and there just after getting out of the car.

"Isn't it a bit too early for you to be out?" I said intending for sarcasm. "Too early for me or too late for you both?" He said. "Now, get back in and I hope you got what you were there for." He added. "Shh, a bit lower, she's still asleep and yeah we did manage to get something even out of that nothingness. "You'll… ac…." I was about to say when he said, "Bro, we aren't that formal are we? We can discuss that inside with a cup of coffee. Now come on in."

"Coming right in, keep a few shots of espresso ready while I get all freshened up." I said. "Roger that." He said and went in.

Y'know when you see a person who's casually just falling asleep when you're around, it's not the fact that they're too lazy at doing the chores, the actual reason for it is that they feel safe when you're around. And if someone is actually holding you tight while doing that, you get to know that the inner child of that person trusts you more than anyone else.

As I looked at her, sleeping like a small child, I couldn't help but feel a sense of awe at her beauty. Her features were delicate, like a porcelain doll, and her brunette hair spilled over my arm like gentle waves.

Despite her beauty, there was a certain childishness to her, especially when she was sleeping. She clung to me like a small child, seeking comfort and security in my embrace.

Her breaths were slow and steady, and I could feel the rise and fall of her chest against my own. It was as if we were one, connected in a way that transcended words or actions.

I couldn't help but smile as I looked 0at her, a smile escaping my lips. She was so innocent, so pure, that it was hard to imagine her ever being anything other than a child.

And yet, there was a strength and resilience to her that belied her childish exterior. She was a fighter, at least for me. Determined to carve out her own path in the world, no matter the obstacles that stood in her way. Or in mine.

As I held her close, I knew that I was lucky to have her in my life. She was my light, my inspiration, and my reason for living. And I would do anything to protect her, to cherish her, and to make her happy for the rest of our days.

I lifted her up gently in my arms, cradling her close to my chest. She stirred slightly, her eyelids fluttered, but then settled back into a deep slumber.

I carried her into the manor, through the hallway with everyone aweing at us, until we reached our room. I placed her carefully on the soft bed, tucking the covers around her.

As I looked down at her, my heart swelled with love and affection. She was so beautiful, so innocent.

I leaned down and pressed a gentle kiss to her

forehead, whispering words of love. She was asleep yet smiled. I suppose she heard me even in her sleep. Ah! My Muffin.

I stood up and turned to leave the room. When I reached the doorknob, I took a glance at her, still sleeping with no fear of the outside world that awaits us every second. Just down the hallway, I found the rest of the team sitting on the couch waiting for me.

"Hey man! How are you feeling today?" Auromic said. "All good, I did have a great sleep though." I said. "Umm, great? Sleeping on the porch in this season isn't great, it's ridiculous!" He said. "Well, that depends on the person who's with you." I said. "I know that it feels great to gaze at the starry night in solitude but have never experienced it with someone else." He said. "Well, now you know what's the difference between great and magical." I said.

"Now, umm… guys, hear me out!" I said. "We sure went to get more about the past. Yet we ended up finding a sweet stalker." I added.

"A what?" Deepak said. "Yep, a stalker. It seems a bit bookish, but the previous owner of the mansion supposedly stalked me." I said. "I know you don't believe in all this, but I did get visions, blurred ones which tried to pin the connection between me and the house." I added.

"Okay, let's just try to blend in. Can you tell us what made you think of all this?" Auromic said. "You remember my VW?" I said. "The black one?" He said.

"Yeah, that one. It was parked, or should I say kept in the garage of that mansion. It still had my belongings which implies, someone preserved it. And not only that, there were newspapers about the accident that caused all the chaos." I said.

"Umm… okay, so if we do see this as a case of stalking, it might be possible that the person was not a stalker at all. They were actually trying to bring things to people. Maybe why exactly all of that happened." Deepak said.

"Are you trying to say that the owner was somehow related to me and was trying to dig out the truth?" I said.

"Yes, exactly. And that also proves that they were a writer and the newspapers tell that the person was working in that company." He said.

"But I found a few things that were actually really close to me in the past years." I said. "Well, maybe they did research on everything that you went through and maybe he thought you were right in all those years." said a voice from my back.

"Sruti, you up already?" I said looking at her.

"You left me alone upstairs, I have told you numerous times that I do fall asleep in your presence, once you get out of the zone, my sleepiness goes away too." She said.

I smiled and shook my head slowly, she raised her eyebrows and crossed her hands.

"Now, coming to the point, the person we all are

here for is supposedly a writer or an editor of a newsdaily and maybe they found a story with a big headline for their paper. They supposedly were obsessed with everything that was happening to you, and kept a record of all the things that were somehow related to you." She said.

"Hmm, that justifies all the polaroids, the newspapers and even the wallpaper of that room. They were actually trying to be me and feel what I was going through." I said.

"Yep. And maybe they did manage to meet you by any chance?" She said. "How will I know?" I said and started thinking of the possible encounters that I had in the past years.

Chapter: 20

I came back to my room without saying a word to anyone. I opened the door and pulled the armchair to the window and stared at the blue sky before me, my mind racing with thoughts of my stalker or so called the writer. I prefer calling them my stalker instead. It seems like a funny thing to have a stalker but when you realise that there was a person spying around me in all those years… it's really spine chilling.

I couldn't shake the feeling that I might have seen them before, that I knew them from somewhere, but I couldn't put my finger on where.

I closed my eyes and took a deep breath, trying to calm myself. I knew that I needed to think clearly if I was going to figure out who my stalker was.

I started to mentally review the past few years, trying to recall any encounters with suspicious individuals. Well, the thing about stalkers is, they actually blend with the normal crowd which makes it near to impossible to have an eye on.

Had I seen anyone lurking around my apartment

building? Had anyone followed me home from work? Had there been any strange phone calls or emails? Well, all of them had a yes on to their answers. As I went through some of the grueling things in my past.

As I traveled through my memories, trying to solve a puzzle, a few cases started to stand out in my mind. The parcel that I once got after some spam emails. I quickly unlocked my phone to see if that did happen or was it just a fake memory.

But were any of them my stalker? I couldn't say for sure. The images were hazy, the details vague. I needed more information, more clues.

With a sigh, I did go back years ago. 2020, that's it. Of what I remember, it was three years ago when I did experience something strange but somehow had forgotten it.

To my surprise, there were no emails in that complete lot. There wasn't even a single one that said 2020. Maybe there was something I had missed. Now, this raised suspicion as it was never possible to have no emails and that to be from a specific year that I was searching for. It was as if someone erased all my emails before I could even think of retrieving them.

"But how is this even possible? Someone just got into the cloud and deleted all the mails." I said to myself and started to scroll through the endless streams of messages and notifications.

Nothing. There wasn't even a single text message from that year.

What if they were someone I knew, someone who was already in my life? The thought was chilling, but it made sense. After all, who else would have the kind of access and information they seemed to possess?

I leaned back and closed my eyes again, trying to calm my racing thoughts. I knew that I needed to be careful, to be vigilant, but I also knew that I couldn't let my fear control me. I just had it in my mind that I would find out who my stalker was.

"Hey! You alright?" Sruti said.

I turned my head towards her and nodded slowly.

"Did you find something?" She said and gave a back hug.

"Umm, nothing till now." I said with a gasp. "Don't you think you should ask someone?" She said while playing with my hair. "Wait… you're right. I can ask Savyy about it." I said and started texting.

… *"Heyy!"* I texted.

… *"Yo!! wassup?"* It read.

… *"Umm, I am kinda in an emergency! Can you help me out with it?"* I texted.

… *"Alright, if I can, I will… lmao!"* It read.

… *"Well, I was thinking if you remember anything suspicious that happened to me back in 2020."* I texted.

… *"Dude, everything that happened to you was suspicious. It was damn 2020!!"* It read.

… *"I'm serious right now, I think I had a stalker lurking around."* I texted.

… *"Makes sense though. But is there anything specific?"* It read.

… *"Yeah, I actually have a blurred memory of something related to emails?"* I texted.

… *"Ohh, emails! Well, it might be a lot of things but is it the 'repleh snatas' thing? You were really worried about that one!"* It read.

… *"The what?"* I texted.

… *"You must have forgotten, you used to say someone was watching you and was sending you emails with something you called 'the altered reality' of some sort. And also mentioned your sister and brothers going down for a party of some sort."* It read.

… *"Oh.. okay.."* I texted.

… *"You alright?"* It read.

… *"Yeah, kinda in a situation right now. I'll keep you posted."* I texted and kept the phone.

"I was right!" I said. "How and why?" She said. "I did manage to know something about them, in the past years yet somehow my memories blurred out!" I said. "So you're saying, you knew you had a stalker?" She said. "Well, not exactly a stalker but a person who was mentally ill." I said. "Umm what?" She said. "There was a person who randomly sent emails, hundreds of them telling me about things of the future." I said.

"And you believe they are actually about to happen or something?" She said. "No! I don't and neither did back then. Because, as far as I remember, it was all a part of a nightmare and as per the psychiatrist, it was caused due to the unfortunate turn of events. Few things that frightened me, did confront me and what I did was, I built completely different stories with characters representing my emotions." I said. "Well, that's what the doc said." I added.

She stood there with confusion. "Hey, don't think about it, it gets complicated when you do." I said. "Okay, I won't think about it but will you be able to find them?" She said. "It's not about finding them, it's about dodging them from their ink stained pages." I said. "Why are you saying this?" She said with confusion. "Well, they're still writing all of it, even at this moment." I said.

"You now are giving me some serious chills, are we gonna be okay?" she said with a bit of tension. "Yeah, we will, they just write, they don't define." I said.

Chapter: 21

With all the thinking and searching things, I completely lost track of time, the sun was ready with its path to set and paint it all with tints of orange.

"The only thing that feels good about today is this. The master stroke of nature. The blend of magnificence. The tones of pleasure." I said to myself.

It was a moment of pure magic, a time when the world seemed to slow down and everything became still. It was a reminder that even in the midst of chaos and uncertainty, there was still beauty to be found, if only I took the time to look for it. As the sun slipped below the horizon, I felt a sense of peace wash over me, and I knew that no matter what happened next, I would always remember this moment of perfect stillness and beauty.

"Hey, lost within the clouds again?" She said. "I sure am. But then somehow the uncertainties find a way to me." I said. "They sure will, everything is kinda messed up right now and now that you know you were somehow close to finding that person in the past years, that might be having a lot of impact on you." She said.

The more I thought about it, the scarier it was. Little did I know I was standing just there, within the reach of a person who supposedly was a stalker and the thing that made my heart pound was that the memories attached to it were all blurred.

"Ahem… you left me hanging there." She said. "Huh?" I said. "Ah yeah, that's correct." I added. "Okay, what's correct?" She said with a smile. "Hehe, sorry I was taken aback by my own thoughts." I said. "It's okay, I get it." She said.

"What now?" She said.

"I think we can't help it. Right now, it is what it is. No matter how much we try, we won't find them and even won't be able to stop them as they are ahead of us in every single action." I said. "Wait! Do you feel like we are taking intervals between the moments we talk? As if someone is putting words into us?" I added.

"Well, now that you have said it, you made me cautious about it." She said.

Someday or the other, we do feel like we speak and do things as if someone has already decided for them to happen.

A simulation?

Maybe. But it might as well indicate that someone has actually seen things beforehand and they might be trying to manipulate things like adding someone unexpected who might have ended up with someone else had they been a bit kinky about it.

"Are you gonna be sitting like this for the rest of the day?" She said. "I mean yeah maybe if you do that too but on me." I said and smirked. "Haha, nice try, now get up, let's get downstairs. I think the sky and the ambiance is just too beautiful and it'll be disrespectful if we ignore it by just sitting inside." She said.

"Yeah, but don't ya think we should tell the cops about it?" I said. "About what the beautiful sky? umm naa, it's better if it's just between the two of us." She said and pulled my hands and made me go out with her.

No sooner than we stepped outside the porch, I could feel the change of worlds. The dark and dull world filled with miseries was taken over by a world filled with colours and peace. The chilled ambiance was taken down by the warmth of the setting sun.

The light was soft and diffused, casting a warm glow over the landscape, and the air was filled with the sweet scent of flowers and the sounds of birds settling down for the night.

We stood there stuck in time.

Not even having a single thought of what was happening or what had happened that caused chaos within ourselves.

I felt a warm flush spread through me at her words.

"I love you." She said, looking into my eyes. "I love this moment and I love the time we spend together."

I smiled back and kissed her forehead. "I love you more." I said. "And I promise to always cherish these moments with you, under the setting sun or wherever life takes us." I added.

"See? How beautiful we both are. Stopping by nature and feeling the presence of a loved one makes everything fade away." She said.

"Umm, yeah but not the stalker though. They are still writing." I said with a grin.

"Oh… stop it Marshy! You know what? We need a break from all this." She said. "Well, that's true, we did manage to pull two researches in this month. The whole team needs a break." I said.

"Yeah, sure the whole team. Why not?" She said and air quoted the whole. "Awe, my Muff. Hey you know what? I'll just have a talk with the firm and let's see if at all we can have a vacation next week. What's say?" I said.

"That would be so relaxing. Please do that. Pleaaassee." She said. "Okay, okayy. Vacation request is on!" I said. "Haha, why are we the four year olds in this team?" she said and giggled.

"Well, sometimes it's better to live like one." I said.

"Ah! I really hope we will be like this forever." She said and snuggled next to me. I wrapped her in my arms and made her rest her head on my shoulder.

Chapter: 22

With a gruesome history of the mansion, we all started to think over the ways we could restore the aesthetics of that beauty.

This, that and what not. Everyone was like let's make it a bit eerie from outside yet heartwarming from the inside. Little did we know, what we were about to create was gonna unfold one of the biggest truths that people usually put a mask on.

Now that everyone knew that I was gonna write for a vacay, there was a sudden increase in the workflow.

Eh, we all are the same aren't we? Burning some more midnight fuel just to get the appraisals.

It is a bit common amongst all, the people always work hard to get their break and yet they don't see how hard they try for it. If one can do things that fast when they think about a vacay in between working tirelessly for months then the only thing that people need is motivation for being what they're supposed to be.

But it is what gives people their identity, that is

how a person gathers courage to do what they are here for. For a few, it is passion and for others it is just another add on to their list of doings. Coming from a country where pursuing passion comes to be a dream of a certain mass, I was one of the lucky ones who could actually get to do what I wanted. But that didn't end there, there are far more difficulties in between. The fight against the stereotype of the minds of others provoking me. The people who think their experience is what defines the world. Is it like that? I never think of it alike.

Everything was on its pace and we were far ahead of our schedule. And the designs were looking gorgeous. The new look was somehow giving us the same vibe yet it had a touch of ours to it.

We are good at imagining things, so yeah, the physical work hadn't started yet. But the designs and concepts were finlised and were ready to be sent for the work to begin. Everything was in the right direction. Every single bit of it.

"No redos eh?" Deepak said. "Haha, no redos and no more 'it could be better' comments." I said.

I went back to my room to check on my phone. It wasn't there. The moment I turned back at the door. Sruti was standing right in front of me.

"So, we are kinda getting into it. And we are fast." She said. "But don't you like it slow?" I said. "Hmm, why don't you check it for yourself." She said and grinned. "Uh… how exactly." I fumbled. "You wanna see? Ahhaan?" She said and started getting close.

She kissed my ear and softly pulled it with her lips. "I love you." She said and looked into my eyes. She held my gaze when I pinned her against the wall.

"You're mine." I said softly, pressing myself into her depths. "Mine alone, now and forever. Mine, whether you will it, or not." She pulled against my grip, and sucked in her breath.

"If you want me to stop, tell me now," I whispered. When she still said nothing, I brushed my mouth against hers. "Or now." I traced the line of her cheekbone. "Or now." My lips were against hers.

I started kissing down her lips, starting with her neck and then further. She tried to resist for a while but then started to get along with it. I kneeled down and kept her legs on my shoulders. "I'll fall over." She said with a gasp. "You won't." I said and started feeling her from inside.

I tasted her for the very first time. She rolled her eyes up at her head and played with my hair. I looked at her and she looked back. She nodded with a gesture to get in. I lifted her up with her clinged on to me by my waist and took her in. We made out again and again with her thirsty enough for more of it.

Eh… you really thought that happened? No! I said she's ticklish! Oh C'mon, read between the lines. She didn't even get past the kiss. Haha.

I did get you there. Didn't I? Lol.

"What? Don't give me that look." She said. "Yeah

sure, why not?" I said, shaking my head slowly. "You know me na? These things aren't for me. Y'know?" She said. "Ah… yeah, you aren't made for those things. Yeah, correct." I said. "Rude." She said slowly. "Say that again?" I said. "You're rude!" She exclaimed. "Me? Rude? Ah… wait…" I said and started to tickle her. "No… no… sorry, aannn… don't." She said while she was trying to resist me tickling her.

"Huh! Thought so." I said and squinched my eyes.

"Bleh bleh.. so…" She said mimicking me.

"What?" I said and started to run after her to tickle her more.

Rest is history.

Well, no, actually we both got tired and decided to watch a movie marathon together. "Hey fellas, it's the Twilight series. Wanna watch?" I said to others. Everyone agreed to it and all of us sat down together at the home theatre and watched the series the whole night.

Well sometimes, sweetness overpowers the spice. I hope you're old enough to know what's the pun here.

Chapter: 23

My eyes opened to the ending song of Zindagi na Milegi Dobara, my all time favourite. I looked around and found that everyone was asleep. With those drowsy eyes, I could see her snuggled all in with her head on my tummy. She was literally hugging it.

Of all the happiness and harmony surrounding me there was still a thought, even though it was a bit awkward yet was convincing. A person who just kept seeing me, feeling what I once did and doing it to themselves, isn't that a thing which most teens do?

It was as if someone likes a celeb and tries to follow their regular chores. But I wasn't anyone with that net worth. So why me?

My phone chimed.

There was an unread message from Savyy.

… *"Dude, we saw adverts here that your firm is restoring a mansion with a mythical significance."* It read.

… *"Haha, mythical significance? I think someone hired a kid as the editor."* I texted.

... *"How's the work?"* It read.

... *"Umm, pretty much of it, is already over. I won't bore you with technical and architectural details. But yeah, 80% of the work is done here.* I texted.

... *"That's great to hear. By the way, who was this built for? Like who owned it before?* It read

... *"I too am confused about it. We were given this project by the local government here. But weren't informed of anything about the previous owner. According to the locals, it was some writer who used to live here but when we dug deep, we found that the writer was some sort of stalker of mine."* I texted.

... *"Whoa! That's a lot to take in. But did you find anything specific to them? Like a picture or something?"* It read.

... *"We did visit the place a couple of times, but there weren't any pictures related to the owner of the house, not like there weren't any. There was actually a lot to filter people out."* I texted.

... *"Don't you think you should use your ability to see things in here?* It read.

... *"Dude, are you trying to ridicule me? This ain't funny, it feels painful when I have those."* I texted.

... *"I wasn't even trying to do that. I am genuinely asking you to see if you can know more about them. Like you once did back then."* It read.

... *"So, this is true then, I can actually experience things *from the way they are settled in and it is not new but it's been there with me for years."* I texted.

... sent an attachment

... "What's it? Why did you send a pic of yours in an off-style jacket from the 80s?" It read.

... "It is the picture I found in a room of the mansion. I didn't show it to anyone though. As I don't get it. I never took this picture. So how on earth is it possible to have this thing in a mansion that I never visited earlier?" I texted.

... "Whoa! Are you trying to loop these events? Like the way things happened back in 2020?" It read.

... "I don't want to do anything, it is too complicated to even correlate to anything of the past." I texted.

... "So according to you, it was you who actually wrote these things and went in a loop of imagination of events happening with you?" It read.

... "Exactly! And I really think of this as I think something similar has already happened in the past." I texted.

... "Have you told anyone about this?" It read.

... "Tell them what? That everyone's nonexistent? That's not how it works. Everything is real and it's not just in my head. Me, Sruti, the team, the projects, the mansion, everything is real and happening. But my concern about this is whether all of this is in the present or is it still in the past." I texted.

... "And how do you intend to solve that?" It read.

… *"Well, I don't know yet but I know one thing that someone's still writing."* I texted.

… *"What now?"* It read.

… *"I have a theory that the editor is still writing even witnessing what's going on right now.* I texted.

… *"Bud, you need to chill, I think you're overthinking it."* It read.

… *"I know I am. It sounds absurd, I know that too but I think I might be right this time."* I texted.

… *"Listen Bhaumik, I still think you haven't recovered completely from the incidents of past years. I advise you to take a vacay, as the work is making things worse. Just finish what you are doing right now and fly home or somewhere else. That will surely help you and also the people who care about you. We can't lose you to a coma again."* It read.

… *"I'm sorry, you are right. I think I need a break from this, that will surely help me get myself upright."* I texted.

… *"Good. Now, spend some time with her and don't be stupid. Do that for us at least."* It read.

… *"I want to and I sure will. Thanks for that, Savvy."* I texted.

… *"A thanks? Dude you owe me chocolates. Get back here and give them to me."* It read.

… *"Haha, Okayy, I will."* I texted.

… *"Haha, take care… you both."* It read.

… *" :) "* I texted.

Chapter: 24

My phone rang. 'Sruuwu Calling'. It flashed. "Muff?" I said. "Up with the phone already?" She said. "Haha, good morning Muff. Had a convo with Savyy." I said. "Ann, talk to me first. Me!" She said. "Awe, come here." I said and hugged her tight.

I gently rubbed her shoulder. "Let's get some coffee. C'mon, freshen up." I said. "Yaayyy, Marshy's coffee!" She jumped in excitement. "Whoa! whoa! whoa! Calm down. Haha." I said.

I got up from the couch and extended my arm to her. She stood and followed me to the coffee maker. I brewed coffee for both of us and she watched me with a smile on her face.

I smiled back and poured two cups of coffee for both of us. We sat on the armchair, right next to the window. She was sitting over me, locking us both onto the chair. We sipped coffee with silence, letting our presence and the ambiance around to fill the voids.

Give us a day, a week or a month, we will never get bored. Even if we just have to sit back and look at eachother. I can. Umm, okay, we can. Haha.

Suddenly, I got an idea. I looked over at her mischievously and suggested playing a prank on the two Kumbhkarans.

Her eyes lit up with excitement. "Yes, let's do it!" she exclaimed.

I leaned towards her and whispered. She giggled and was ready to give it an action.

We quietly tiptoed back into the home theater, where Auromic and Deepak were still sound asleep. Me and her snuck up and dumped a bucket of ice-cold water on them.

Both of em' shot up in surprise, shivering and wide-eyed. They looked around in confusion, trying to figure out what had happened.

We burst out laughing, feeling a rush of childish glee. "Dude! That's so immature!" Deepak said. "Ahhaan? You want another bucket don't ya?" I said. "No.. no.. sorry…." Before he could finish, I poured another bucket just reserved for this moment. "You want some too? I said. "Ah, No.. thanks. Spare me please." He said. "Haha, chicken." I said.

The four of us spent the rest of the morning joking around and enjoying each other's company, grateful for the simple pleasures of life and the joy of having good friends.

"Few more days and we will be done with all the paperwork." Auromic said. "We also need to inform the firm about the fieldwork that should be carried out before they do as per their own wish." I said. "Everyone needs to be spoon fed. Noone still stands a chance without us being united for it." She said. "Still, we work there, we need to, that's why they pay for us." I said.

"True that, the money seal shuts the reality. Doesn't it?" She said. "Hey, Muff, take it easy. You seem a bit too flustered." I said. "Yeah whatever." She said and stormed off.

I went to get her back.

"Cramps again?" I said. "Yes." She said with a puppy face. "Aww, come here my lil' Hazel." I said and wrapped my arms around her. I also glided my fingers just below her shoulder. It makes her feel better.

I took her in and made her sit with a pillow.

When it comes,

It comes.

"Hey gorgeous, here's something that'll help." I said and gave her a hot water bag with some dark chocolates. It's the cravings that matter. Nothing else. For some, satisfying those cravings can reduce the pain to much extent.

As the day wore on, we decided to take a walk down to the nearby lake. The sun was setting, casting a warm, orange glow over the water. I took her hand and we walked, admiring the beauty of the scenery and the tranquility of our moment.

The vast meadows,

The azure abode,

The bliss of the flowers,

The warmth of love,

All for one,

One for all,

Us.

"Can we stay here forever?" She said. "Like this or like here?" I said. "Both." She said and smiled. "We will always stay like this. And yeah, we already are here, in both of our arms, no second thoughts so yeah that too is forever." I said and gently bumped my head with hers.

As we made our way back to the manor, the air grew cooler, and the stars began to twinkle overhead. We felt a sense of contentment and peace, knowing we did actually spend the day in the best possible way.

Once we were back in the manor, I settled her into bed, exhausted from the day's activities. We cuddled up together, relishing the warmth of each other's embrace.

As we drifted off to sleep, we felt a sense of gratitude for the simple moments we shared with ourselves and the beauty of the world around us. We knew that tomorrow would bring new adventures and new memories, but for now, we were content to bask in the afterglow of a perfect day.

Chapter: 25

I woke up to the warm rays of the sun streaming through the window. I felt a soft hand caressing my cheek and opened my eyes to see Sruti, looking at me with all the love she had. I smiled and pulled her closer, enjoying the warmth of her embrace.

"Good morning, sleepyhead." she whispered, planting a soft kiss on his lips. "Ah! This one time, you got to call me that. Not gonna happen again though." I said and laughed. "Oh, is it? Nor if I make you tired the whole night?" She said with a grin.

"What time is it?" I said rubbing his eyes and with a soft smile.

"Early enough for us to have some fun." She said with a mischievous grin. "But yeah late enough to make us run for the meeting." She said and tapped her wrist. "You know that right? There's no watch there." I said and laughed.

"Uh-huh? Really?" She said. "Why do you sound so flirtatious today?" I said. "You'll see." She said.

She got up and pulled me out of the bed, leading him into the shower.

"Whoa! Someone's on a spree. Thanks to your periods." I said sarcastically. "Shh!" She said and pulled me close to a passionate kiss.

Playful splashes,

Echoing laughs,

Sinister hand movements,

A warm bath.

Ahem.

"It was something different." I said when we got out. She put on her robe and said, "Are you complaining?" "Uhh… n…nooo! It was beautiful. Unique." I said fumbling. "Haha, look at you. You're so cute." She said. I stood there with a stupid smile.

"Now, c'mon, we need to hurry. The meet starts at quarter past ten." She said and went to her walk in closet. "I almost forgot about it. Are the other guys up yet?" I said. "Maybe? I don't know. My guy is up. That's what I can say." She said. I smiled and got back to my room to get dressed.

I got out in about 10 minutes and just as I locked my door I heard the sound of heels clicking on the hardwood floor. It was her walking towards him in a breathtakingly beautiful gown that hugged her curves in all the right places. Her hair was styled perfectly, cascading down her back in soft waves, and her makeup was flawless.

I felt my breath catch in my throat as I took in the sight before me. I had seen Sruti in many different outfits, but this one was something special. It was as if she had transformed into a goddess, radiating confidence and beauty.

The gown was a deep shade of emerald green that complemented her skin tone perfectly, and it had a slit that revealed a hint of her toned legs.

"You look amazing!" I said with my eyes locked on her. She stood there smiling. "So do you, sweetheart." She said and leaned, planting a soft kiss.

"C'mon, let's go." I said and took her arm in mine. We went down the hallway and saw the team was ready too. "Wow! you two look drop dead gorgeous!" Auromic said. "Thanks man. You look classy as always!" I said. "Where's Deepak going?" I added. "Oh, he forgot to wear his cologne." He said. "Oh, there he is, our dashing prince." I said. "Stop it now, you guys." Deepak siad. "Let's go, we need to make it in ten." He added. "Don't worry, we'll make it in five." I said and turned towards the front yard.

We had our beauties ready. A cool stone continental GT and a tuscan flying spur. "Absolute masterpiece of mankind." I said. "Agreed." Auromic said. "I call the GT." I said. "Okay, the spur's mine. Give me the sheets, I've more space." He said. "Cool, let's roll out." I said after giving them to him.

I took her to the car and opened the door for her. Having everything settled down, the beast was ready to roll.

I started the engine. The V8 yelled British in every language. "Let's go!" I said and hit the gas.

We drove to the mansion. It wasn't what I expected it to be. As there were a lot of exotic cars parked right in front. "It seems like a pretty big deal." I said. "Seems like this mansion is gonna be painted with money." Sruti said.

"We parked the Bentleys and started approaching the crowd. As we entered, we were greeted by a whole bunch of people, including the press and the senior firm members.

You know about the big debut everyone cries for? This was it. For me, for us, for everyone present here.

We went to the stage and were ready for our hard work to click on.

Me and my team presented our designs for the renovation project, showcasing their creative vision and attention to detail.

It was a protracted session mixed with loud chatters and voiceless minutes.

When we finished, there was a moment of silence, and then the senior firm members started clapping. The applause spread, and soon everyone in there was clapping and cheering.

We had done it – our design was accepted and praised. The government officials were happy that we as a team of four young adults could rekindle the vintage with the city's new tone.

Overwhelmed with emotion, I hugged her tightly. We all celebrated our success. It was an hour later when we were having some drinks toasting to our success, when the founder of our firm reached out to me.

"Bhaumik! Your team did it again. That's why you guys are my precious platinum." He said.

"It's just hard work sir. No selfless pride, just hard work." I said and extended my hand for a firm handshake.

He shook his hands and gave me an envelope. He didn't say anything and just left. I sat down at the table with everyone looking at me with suspicion. "Guys, I don't know what's inside. Don't look at me like I'm Brutas. Let's see." I said and cut open the envelope.

" To my dearest team,

It was all you and your tireless efforts made us have a deal worth a big shot.

Without you guys, we won't have made it through. Here, I raise my toast to you and not just that, our firm is rewarding you with a much-needed vacation – a chance to relax and enjoy your accomplishment.

The big break you always deserved."

All of us looked at him, he had raised a toast for us. And showed us the birds sign to boast about the fact that he knows about me and her.

We raised our glasses so that he could see. We looked at each other and smiled at our project and the big break that came with it.

Chapter: 26

All these months of hard work and now we part ways. All of us had packed our bags and were outside the manor we were living in. "Y'know, there's always this connection we get with the places we have been to, the moment we share in it becomes unforgettable." I said. "True to its very core. We have defined places for a really long time but we also do get that back from them." Sruti said. "Well, that's what life is all about, any good done by someone, comes back to them at some point of time." Auromic added.

There was a brief pause, and everyone looked at Deepak. "What? You expect me to say something emotional dedicated to the manor? Uh-nah, I'll pass. You guys do the Oxford thing, I'll focus on the snack bars on my route." He said and went back to surf on his phone.

Everyone laughed at this.

"So, we part again. Of course for a while. Let's see if we get to work together next time." I said. "We will, I hope he keeps us with the same affection that he has for us." Deepak said. "I'm sure he will, given for our hardships, we sure are a great team." She said.

We smiled at that. "So, any particular vacation schedules?" I said. "Umm, for me, I'm gonna go back home and spend some time with my wife and the kids." Auromic said. "Ah, that feels so great, how's Aditi by the way?" I said. "She's good, she is really excited to see me back. I was actually on a call with her minutes back." He said. "Hmm, someone's a secret romantic." I said. "There's nothing to do with any secret romance, its just not everyone is as lucky to have a girlfriend in the same field as one's." He said. "Aww, I smell something burning." I said. "Dudes, cut it out!" Deepak said. Sruti was laughing at the back.

"Does it have to be like the last episode of friends?" Auromic said. "Why does every end sound wholesome yet sad. Everyone loves the journey, why can't every journey continue in a loop?" He added.

"Because every journey has its destination, even in books, every path you choose, leads you to an alternate reality." I said.

"A part of the journey is the altered reality?" Sruti said. "Ah! Someone has read the book." I said.

"Yes I did. Didn't I?" Auromik and Deepak said in chores. "Haha, nice try guys, nice try. But guess who made it through." I said and smirked. "Smirking won't help you get the greens back." Deepak said. Everyone laughed at it. All but me.

I made a great loser face and stared at him. "Don't use x-ray vision on me, I'm a man, use it over there." He said and laughed. "Total jerks." I said and turned away. "Oh c'mon dude, how much we missed you after college? You left without saying goodbye. There were few of the roasts we saved for you." He said.

"I'm sorry too, you're right. I should've stayed a bit after graduation. How's everyone?" I said. "On the last day when we are about to leave for a vacay, you ask about your college buds? Dude." He said.

"Well, I didn't have a nice college life, did I?" I said. "Nice? Dude, you were filled with stardom at college. Everyone knew you and were obsessed with befriending you." He said. "Befriend me for what? For the person I was or the name I got from all the stardom?" I said. "That's what always mattered to me. I never had real friends there. Except for the few." I said.

Well, yeah, it wasn't just limited to my college days, I was a kid who never had friends. It was pretty hard from the start. Being from a strict household, I was always required to be present indoors, and doing so cut me off from hangouts with anyone from school. I used to have cycle buddies in the neighbourhood but with time, we lost touch. It was really hard to cope with all this but the only thing that helped me feel better in solitude was my grandma.

It wasn't until I turned 18, I lost her. I still remember she had a smile on her face when she passed away. That took away a lot from me which in turn made everything a lot more difficult. Back then I called myself a lost teen. And the only thing that has changed after that is the 'teen'.

Chapter: 27

"Umm, guys, why does it feel like the awkward silence has been continuing for ages?" Sruti said. "That's probably because I've been like that for ages." I said. "Heyy, don't act all sad, I'm here with you na… Let's go, c'mon. Forget all that for a while and let's go." She said and extended her hand. I slid my hand right in.

She took my hand and raised it up. "Now woosh! Turn around." She said. I analysed this for a bit. "Dude, you're supposed to do that. Not me." I said. "Why? Stop being stereotypical." She said. "It's not stereotypical, it is how things are done. And I get it." I said. "Get what?" She said. "I get it that you don't consider yourself as a girl. At least seeing you trim the moustache." I said and laughed. "Youuuuuuuu! Come here right now!" She said and started to chase me. We were running around the front yard with Deepak and Auromic giggling about the joke I cracked. It was all fun.

She stopped running in the middle and looked down. I looked at her and said, "Hey, hey… what's wrong bunny." "Nothing." She said in a low voice. I ran back to her and held her by her shoulders.

"Hey look at me, what's wrong hon?" I said. "You teased me for my looks. I know I don't look good." She said. "Whoa! Hey… you're the most beautiful girl I've ever met. I love every single thing about you." I said and hugged her. "Annn… no you don't." She said. "Yes I do. I do love everything about you. Everything, even your moustache." I said and didn't let my laugh slip through my lips. "Ann… you're mean!" She said and pulled herself away. "Awe, sorry, sorry, don't forget that I am your best friend too, so all the teasing and extreme perks do come with me. Whatever I say, whatever I do, always remember that it'll forever be us, me and you." I said and gave her a gentle kiss.

"See? I can't even be mad at you, where do you manage to keep this cuteness when I'm not around?" She said. "Hmm, that's a really nice question. Why don't you ask the other girls who work around me?" I said. "Annn, I'm not talking to you." I said. "Haha, really?" I said. "Yes!" She said. "Okay then, bye" I said and started walking away. "Annn." She said and ran towards me.

"You're not going anywhere! Not without me. I won't let you do that!" She said and climbed on my back and crossed her leg locking herself at my waist. "Ask the other girls.. right? Wait till I take care of them by myself. I'll make them forget the ways to compliment guys. You're mine! And that's it!" She said.

I laughed a lot and tried not to topple down to the ground as she was on top of me.

"Okay kids, it's time to go. Do you have your ID or should we hire a babysitter who can take you on your vacation?" Deepak said. "Ha-ha-ha, not funny." She said.

"Muff, let's get going, come down hon." I said kneeling down for her to get down. "No! That's the punishment, carry me to the car, I'm a small baby. I can't walk." She said. "Ohh, are you? Then you must be pretty good at learning things fast." I said. "Why?" She said. "Well, babies don't shout deeper in the morning unless someone tells a story to hide treasury in their favourite sandcastle on a beach." I said and gave a mischievous grin.

"Ahem, I'm a baby, that's it. I don't know what the conventional one's are equipped with. But yeah I have all that. Take it or leave it." She said and turned her face to the other side.

"Haha, my lil' Hazel. My sweet Muffin." I said and smiled. I carried her till my car and put her in the passenger seat.

"Farewell amigos!" I said to them and sat in the car. I rolled the windows down and bade a good bye. We revved our engines and started to move.

Our cars went in two different directions knowing that someday, we'll meet again.

Soon, it sometimes is a pun.

Might be tomorrow,

Or the day after,

Even months from now,

And sometimes,

Never.

Chapter: 28

"Whoa! Easy there hon." She said. The gear shaft somehow got stuck in the middle for a while. Which in turn made me shift down once and shift up again. "Eh, don't worry, I've seen worse things happening and got out. This is nothing." I said.

"Umm... mister, I think you've someone here with you. And perhaps you should drive carefully for that reason? And maybe just don't say anything?" She said. "I'm sorry hon. I got carried away." I said and made sure to give a full clutch.

"Look at the trees! They look so beautiful. Heyy, don't run away from us, run with us." She said to the trees. I smiled and said, "The moment they do that, would be the last one for us." I said and laughed.

Just like a bird flying smoothly with the cool breeze, we drove down the road. I looked at her.

Her hairs, swinging slowly like the waves of a calm ocean, softly framing her face as she looked out the window, lost in thought. I reached out and gently brushed a strand of hair behind her ear, revealing the softness of her skin.

She turned to me, a smile playing on her lips. "What is it?" she asked.

"Nothing." I said, shaking his head. "Just admiring the view."

She raised an eyebrow, a mischievous glint in her eye. "And what view might that be?" she asked.

I grinned, taking her hand in mine. "The most beautiful view in the world." I said, bringing her hand to my lips and placing a gentle kiss on her knuckles.

She blushed, her cheeks turned to a tint of rose. "You always know just what to say." she said, her eyes shining with affection.

I leaned over and pressed a soft kiss on her forehead. "I mean it." I said with my voice barely above a whisper. "You are the most beautiful thing I have ever seen."

She leaned her head against my shoulder, and I gave a soft pat on her head, she held the gearshift and I held her hand as we drove down the road. The sun began to set, painting the sky in a riot of colors, but for me, there was only one thing he could see - her eyes, shining like jewels in the fading light.

As we strolled through the bustling streets of the quaint coastal towns, I couldn't help but feel a sense of contentment wash over myself. Hand-in-hand with her, we explored every nook and cranny, indulging in local delicacies and immersing themselves in the vibrant festivals that filled the air with music and laughter. From the breathtaking views atop the lighthouse to the lively night markets that illuminated the streets, every moment was savored and cherished. With each passing day, we grew closer, sharing secrets and making memories that would last a lifetime. It was as though time had stood still, allowing us to reveal the joy of each other's company and the beauty of their surroundings. For us, this vacation was nothing short of a dream come true.

"Way to go hon." I said. "The fantasies we imagined all along, we are finally fulfilling them. I'm so happy." She said.

As we drove along the winding road, we spotted a bridge at a distance. "I've never seen that one before." I said and without hesitation, I turned the car and made our way towards it. As we got on the bridge, we were struck by the serene beauty of the water below and the sky above. The gentle breeze ruffled our hair, and we both let out a contented sigh.

"This is amazing, you're amazing, we are amazing!" she said, looking out at the water below.

"I know." he replied, a smile on his face. "It's like we're the only ones in the world right now."

I parked the car at the end of the bridge and got out, taking in the view of the water stretching out before us. We sat on the railing, enjoying the moment in each other's company.

I turned to her, taking her hand in mine. "You know what?" I said. "I feel like we could stay here forever."

She smiled, leaning her head on my shoulder. "Me too." she said. "This is perfect." "We are." I added.

As we sat there, watching the water flow beneath us, we both felt a sense of peace and contentment wash over each other. In that moment, we knew that we were exactly where we were meant to be, together on this bridge, lost in our own little world.

The sun began to set, casting a warm glow over the water, and we watched as the sky turned a deep shade of orange and pink. We stayed there until the last bit of light faded from the sky, reluctant to leave this magical place.

As we made their way back to the car, I turned to her with a smile. "You know what?" I said. "I think we just found our new favorite spot."

She laughed, leaning in to kiss him. "I couldn't agree more." she said. "This is our spot, and no one can take it from us." She added.

The stars started to lit the night sky. It was magical! We rolled down the windows and felt the wind rush through. We looked at each other. "Isn't this what we always wanted?" I said. "Yes! You, me, us, this place, under the night sky." She said. I smiled at her and she smiled back. "Muff, could you check the maps for the nearest motel?" I said. "Let's take some time off for a nap and we will continue our adventure tomorrow." I said. "What's say?" She said. "Yeah, well let's save a few fantasies for the next day." She said.

She took out her phone. "Well, the nearest hotel is

back there. Like we have to take a u-turn." She said and pointed towards the other side of the bridge. "Umm, okay, let's get going then. C'mon sweetheart, guide us through!" I said. She laughed and said, "Such a drama y'know."

I revved the engine and started the car. It was getting late and the fog had taken over the night skies. It was getting kinda eerie. A night on a bridge with silence roaring through the winds.

As we drove down through the thick blanket of fog that descended upon us, it started to feel a bit nauseous as the fog was obscuring my vision and making it difficult to navigate. Suddenly, the car's untuned gearshift made it race against the upcoming fog and we hit a median at the center of the road. It caused it to skid uncontrollably before plunging into the icy waters below.

"Muff, you alright?" I said and looked at her as the car started to sink down to the river. "I think I hurt my head." She said sobbing. "You're bleeding!" I said and quickly tied my handkerchief on it to stop it from oozing further. "I think I'm losing my sense. Marshyyy… Marshy, you hear me?" she said. "I can hear something." As she stumbled through the fog, she could barely make out the red and blue lights of the ambulance that arrived on the scene, their sirens piercing the eerie silence. "Don't worry, we will be fine." She said and held my hand.

She probably couldn't see but I somehow had opened up her seat belts and made her get out of the car. The only thing that was left with me was the blurred vision of her floating to the top of the surface and for me, it was the dark coloured icy water that took me in.

Chapter: 29

"I opened my eyes to a blur of flashing lights and panicked voices. My head was pounding, and I felt like I was floating. I tried to move, but my body wouldn't respond. It was as if I was paralyzed." She said.

"Out of nowhere, a voice said stay with us, sweetie. You're going to be okay… I heard him, it was him. I can never be wrong in identifying his voice." She said and sobbed.

"It sounded far away yet so close to my heart. I tried to speak, call out my love for him but my throat felt like it was on fire." She said.

Suddenly, I was being lifted onto a stretcher, and was being rolled through a maze of corridors. Doctors and nurses rushed past me, their faces tense and focused.

"We need to get her into surgery!" One of them said. "We don't have much time."

My heart started to race. Surgery? What'd happened to me? Where's he gone? I can't make it through without seeing him. These were the thoughts piling up in my mind. A sudden urge to just see him and feel his presence made me anxious and frightened at the same time.

The stretcher came to a stop, and now I was wheeled into a bright, sterile room, where a team of doctors and nurses surrounded me, their faces obscured by masks.

"Can you hear me?" One of them asks.

I could hear them but all of the muscles of my face ached and blood covered my eye sight. I did try to nod, but my head feels like it was made of lead.

"We need to put you under anesthesia." The doctor said. "Just count backwards from ten."

"Whe…. where's h…" I tried to but My whispers too couldn't make it past my throat.

I closed my eyes, hoping that everything happening was just a dream. A mere nightmare. He can't leave me here all alone. He's just playing around as he always does. Before I could make something out of what was happening with me, everything went black.

I don't remember anything from there. What happened to me, where I was but most importantly the only thing I could remember was my constant thoughts searching for him. When the darkness consumed me, all I could see was his smile and the way he looked at me when I was down with a cold. All of our time was flashing back at me. All our memories, our fantasies, his childishness and of course his love for me.

When I opened my eyes again, the bright lights of the hospital room were replaced by a dimmer glow. I felt groggy and disoriented, but I could sense that I was not alone.

As my vision cleared, I saw him sitting by my side. Relief washed over me as I realized that he was here. He was always there. Sitting by my side, looking at me, checking whether I was asleep or I needed his warmth for falling into the bliss of the night.

"Hey… Muff!" he said, his voice soft and comforting. "How are you feeling?"

I tried to speak, but my throat was still dry and scratchy. I nodded instead, and he smiled.

"I'm so glad you're alright." he said. "I've been so worried about you. You have been like that for quite a while now sweetheart."

I somehow managed to whisper a response. "I missed you."

He leaned in close, "I have missed you more." he said. "I've been here every day since you were brought in."

I smiled weakly, feeling a sense of warmth and comfort in his presence.

"What happened to me?" I asked all squeaky.

He took my hand and gently rubbed his thumb on my knuckles. "We were in a car accident." He said. "But you're going to be okay. The doctors took care of you."

I tried to sit up, but he gently pushed me back down. "Take it easy." He said. "You need rest."

"Annn… No, I need you!" I said anxiously. "Muff, I'm here right? Now c'mon, have a nice and long nap. It'll heal you well." He said.

I looked at him with tears pouring down my cheeks, "Don't go anywhere. Be here with me. Please?" I said.

He smiled and gently kept his hand on my forehead. He brushed it gently and said, "I love you, you love me, let me be your fantasy, sweetheart, go to sleep."

"I haven't heard that for ages." I said. "Hmm, okay, I'll sing you to sleep. Just like we used to." He said and started humming it.

I nodded and closed my eyes with peace as I knew he was there, My Marshy was there with me. I felt safe and protected, knowing that he's by my side.

Chapter: 30

"I opened my eyes and saw him then and there, he didn't even move an inch. He was there sitting by my side all night, holding my hand so that I won't feel lonely." She said.

"I asked him whether he wanted some coffee. He smiled but didn't say anything. His eyes looked as if they were stuck in time, painful yet happy." She said.

"Just stay here." She said. "I said that to him, he just watched, sitting there looking at me, with the same eyes. I was worried for him, so I took off the cables attached to me and wore the flip flops that were just below the bed."

"They were cold and a bit covered in dust, as if no one wore them for the past few months. I took them and went out of the room. It was a busy corridor with everyone looking at me like they saw a miracle. I still remember one of the nurses saying… you.. you're up! Oh good lord. She said that and started running to the doctor. Within minutes, a small batch of the hospital staff surrounded me. Miss, you were in a coma for the past six years, a doctor said that to me. I was flustered for a bit thinking of the time I was asleep. The moment I regained myself, I rushed into my room with a sudden urge to hug him tight." She said

"But the moment I opened the door, I saw everything, everything was just the way I left a minute before, yet there was one piece missing. Him." She said. "Marshy, marshyyy! Where are you? I cried and weeped for not being able to find him."

The doctor said, "Miss, it's not good for your health. Please sit down miss. Let us check your vitals." "I told them … no! First tell me where he is." She said.

"Where who is ma'am?" One of the staff members said. "Mar… umm, Bhaumik… Bhaumik Mohanty. Where is he? He was just here with me. I went out to bring him a cup of coffee, but when I went back in, he isn't here." She said.

"Meanwhile someone had dialed up to Auromic and Deepak, so they came in to check on me. Where is he? Where is he? Answer me… I kept asking them. Both of them stood still and kept looking with sadness in their eyes. Back there they didn't have the guts to speak the truth. Moments later, Deepak came back with a newspaper with tears in his eyes. What is all this? Can somebody tell me where Marshy is? He was just here with me. We have been talking right from the day I got in here. I kept saying these continuously until Deepak pointed out the headlines of an old newspaper, it was dated 2023 that is six years back in the past. Why are you showing me this? I know it's the same day today and it was the same day on that day too. Before I could ask about him again, my eyes got stitched to a particular line, it read, *'Drowned by the wheel - One survivor left, still in coma.'* There was a small photograph of him right at the bottom of the article. It was that moment when I was stunned. Not a single word, not a single blink, nothing. I froze just as I saw his photograph. Time passed by, both of them went home, but I was there, sitting on the bed holding his photograph in the newspaper." She said.

"All this time, all these years, I was all alone by myself hoping that you still are waiting for me... I said that looking at it. Why Marshy... why? I screamed, I weeped, I cried aloud. Yet no one was there to calm me down, his shoulders that helped me fall asleep were long buried inside the depth of the water. I cried all night holding the pendent he gave me years ago, the only thing that I had of him." She said.

"It went all black again, as if it were my pills that made me drowsy, my vision got blurred, and the only thing I could sense was someone was there again, I love you... You love me ... Let me be your fantasy... Marshyyy? I whispered but I was too tired to keep my eyes open. That was that moment then and this is me now, its been a decade to that incident yet the memories are fresh." She said.

"Whoa! I can't say that I can feel your pain, but I sure can say the pain you took yourself and still do, makes you an epitome of a love which still exists even without the existence of your partner. You two had a tragic past. And I am really sorry for what happened." He said.

"Ah, it's okay but don't say that he doesn't exist. I still wait for him. I still wait for him to pull up his car at the front and wait for me holding the door." Sruti said.

"So, you know the reason why those pages were kept unwritten. He missed out in writing the end to his love. Which shows why I'm still waiting for him. He always mentioned a writer and said they don't define us, they just write." She said.

"That's what we do." He said and smiled.

"You know, you do look like him when you smile. I can't say for sure, all these years have taken the sight to see through people." She said. "I didn't catch your name though."

"Oh… I'm so sorry, with all the tension I had finding his notes and making all the fuss about not finding the rest, I completely forgot to mention my name… I am…" He kept saying but it was all masked within the sights of something that could never have happened.

Sruti ran outside without telling him anything. "Umm, okayy… I just bought the mansion down the road. Incase…. ah nevermind, she's gone." He said.

"That was so serene. Two lovers, separated by nature yet the soul of the deceased still made the other believe in love." He said and bent down to pick a newspaper that fell off her hands while she ran.

It read… *'Six years of healing, yet taken by an old wound - Sruti, the girl who was in coma for six years, got up, healed from her past yet was taken by a severe cardiac arrest after she came to know about the unfolded truth.'*

He stood there in shock. "If she was dead all this time, then who was here telling me the story of her sorrowful love?" He said and while he ran towards the door, he saw someone at the window.

There was a red Mazda parked right in front of the Manor, a man, looking like a young adult, standing by the side of the car, holding the door open. There stood Sruti running towards him and hugging him tight.

She filled him with kisses and he swung her around like two lost souls meeting in the afterlife. There he stopped and placed her down gently. He kissed her forehead and made her sit in the car.

All of this happened in front of this new writer who came here for having a lead on someone he was writing on and now he stood as the part of their lives.

No sooner than he got in the car, the car faded into nothingness. As if they both got what they wanted. A never ending fairytale.

...

Always remember,

Love never ends,

It always grows,

People might think they got solitude,

But nature always knows,

The more one persuades,

The more one retrospects,

Even when everything falls out of one's own mistake,

Even when you feel everything is a pretend,

Always remember,

Love never ends.

Black Eagle Books

www.blackeaglebooks.org
info@blackeaglebooks.org

Black Eagle Books, an independent publisher, was founded
as a nonprofit organization in April, 2019. It is our mission
to connect and engage the Indian diaspora and the world at
large with the best of works of world literature published
on a collaborative platform, with special emphasis on
foregrounding Contemporary Classics and New Writing.